WATERLOO HIGH SCHOOL LIBRARY

P9-CCG-817

WATERLOO HIGH SCHOOL LIBRARY
1464 INDUSTRY RD.
ATWATER, OHIO 44201

# If ANYTHING

WATERLOO HIGH SCHOOL LIBRARY
1464 INDUSTRY RD.
ATWATER, OHIO 44201

# If ANYTHING

## Martha Swearingen

ELSEVIER/NELSON BOOKS
*New York*

Fic
Swe

For my father
JAMES CALVIN McKINNON
1905–1964

with thanks to all who helped me—
Ricci and Dee
Ann, Judy, and Lynda
Fred, Celia, and Dan

No character in this book is intended to represent any actual person; all the incidents of the story are entirely fictional in nature.

Copyright © 1980 by Martha Swearingen
All rights reserved. No part of this publication may be reproduced or transmitted in any form or by any means, electronic or mechanical, including photocopy, recording, or any information storage and retrieval system now known or to be invented, without permission in writing from the publisher, except by a reviewer who wishes to quote brief passages in connection with a review written for inclusion in a magazine, newspaper, or broadcast.

Library of Congress Cataloging in Publication Data

Swearingen, Martha.
  If anything.

  I. Title.
PZ4.S9734If 1979    [PS3569.W353] 813'.5'4    79–25965
ISBN 0–525–66673–7

Published in the United States by Elsevier/Nelson Books, a division of Elsevier-Dutton Publishing Company, Inc., New York. Published simultaneously in Don Mills, Ontario, by Thomas Nelson and Sons (Canada) Limited.

Printed in the U.S.A.    First Edition
10  9  8  7  6  5  4  3  2  1

## ACKNOWLEDGMENTS

Grateful acknowledgement is made to the following individuals or publishers for permission to quote from copyrighted works:

April-Blackwood Music, for lines from "Sweet Baby James" by James Taylor (pp. 154, 207). Copyright © 1970 by Blackwood Music, Inc., and Country Road Music. All rights administered by Blackwood Music, Inc. Used by permission.

Combine Music, for lines from "Loving Her Was Easier" by Kris Kristofferson (p. 71).

Norma Millay Ellis, for lines from "The Return" by Edna St. Vincent Millay (p. 155). From *Collected Poems*, Harper and Row. Copyright 1928, 1955 by Edna St. Vincent Millay and Norma Millay Ellis.

Houghton Mifflin Company, for two quotations from *The Lord of the Rings* by J. R. R. Tolkien (pp. 20, 168). Copyright by Houghton Mifflin Company.

Macmillan Publishing Co., Inc., for lines from "Hillcrest" by Edwin Arlington Robinson (epigraph page). From *Collected Poems* of Edwin Arlington Robinson. Copyright 1916 by Edwin Arlington Robinson, renewed 1944 by Ruth Nivison.

Oxford University Press, for a line from "As Kingfishers Catch Fire" by Gerard Manley Hopkins (p. 79).

Random House, Inc., Alfred A. Knopf, Inc., for lines from two poems by Wallace Steven: "Large Red Man Reading" (p. 79) and "Sunday Morning" (p. 79). Copyright by Alfred A. Knopf, Inc.

Charles Scribner's Sons, for lines from "Luke Havergal" by Edwin Arlington Robinson (p. 19).

Shapiro, Bernstein and Co., Inc., for lines from "The Wreck of the Old 97" by Henry Whitter, Charles W. Noell, and Fred J. Lewey (pp. 124, 223). Copyrights 1924, 1939, 1940, and 1944. Renewed by Shapiro, Bernstein and Co., Inc. New York, New York 10022. Used by permission.

Abner Spector, for lines from "Sally, Go 'Round the Roses" by Abner Spector (p. 82). Copyright by Cherish Music (ASCAP).

Starday Music, for lines from "A Picture from Life's Other Side" by William York (p. 82).

*Who knows to-day from yesterday*
*May learn to count no thing too strange:*
*Love builds of what Time takes away*
*Till Death itself is less than Change.*

—Edwin Arlington Robinson, 1916

# 1

ASHGROVE FRAZIER HAD BEEN PEACEFULLY HAUNTING her old home for some time, when she learned that she was no longer to be the only ghost on the place. An appalling crash—no shriek of brakes, just the crash—jarred the quiet country night and brought her running down to the roadside to see what was wrong. Ashgrove had never been allowed to see violent death. She was just too late to see this one. The small foreign car had missed the curve, slewed around, and smashed against the stone retaining wall that held up her front garden. The headlights were out. But she could see that the body of the driver had been thrown clear. It lay in the tall grass of dry September, face down and still, the head turned at an odd angle into the shoulder.

Someone was standing there beside it: a young man, tall, dark, and untidy, looking bewildered and shocked. Ashgrove looked at him, down at the body, and then up at him again. Then she said, "You'd better come home with me."

The first thing Martin Evans said to her was, "If I'm here, then who's that?"

"It doesn't matter right now," Ashgrove said gently. "Don't worry, not right now, anyway."

"I must have picked up a hitchhiker and don't remember it. I bet I have a concussion. Well, let's see about him." Martin's time in the army was guaranteed to have prepared him for a sight like this or worse, but it was not easy for him to approach the body and stoop over it. "Oh, God." He fought a draining weakness and reluctance, unable to be glad that he himself at least seemed to be unhurt. "He's definitely not breathing. His neck may be broken. But I don't want to touch him and see." He straightened up. "I have to get to a phone."

"You don't recognize him?"

"No. I can't tell much about him. I don't want to lift up his head and look at his face. He has this scalp wound." Dark hair and dark blood obscured the upturned cheek. He could guess without looking that gravel would be ground into the other cheek and more blood would probably be oozing from the slack mouth. That was bad enough, but there was more to his revulsion than that. He turned away from the body and asked again; "Do you have a phone?"

"Are you all right? Are you hurting?"

"I guess I'm all right."

"Come on with me and I'll fix you a cup of tea."

"Get serious. Do you really think I could drink a cup of tea?"

10

"No. But the aroma will do you good."

The last thing Martin had intended was to follow this odd girl who talked in circles. He meant to run up to the main road, wherever it might be, and find help for the unknown dead man and himself, not to mention his car. Her house—what he could see of it—looked uninviting. It hulked up beyond its overgrown hedges, tall and gabled and not a light showing against the moonless sky and the few western stars. But on the chance that she might have a telephone, he walked beside her up the grass-choked ruts of the lane, through the back garden, and into the back door of a big dark kitchen.

She lit a fat smoky candle and appeared as a slight, barefooted figure with short brown hair, wearing tan corduroy pants and a fisherman's sweater. Though she was not pretty, the candlelight was kind to her. In its flickering dimness she might have been any age between twenty and thirty, but for a grown woman she was little, hardly standing over five feet.

"I bet you don't have a phone after all," Martin said.

"Well, I never heard that the C and P gave it away."

"Or any electricity either."

"Or any running water. None of those people give it away. Out here you have to have electricity for running water anyway. I just use the pump. Just a minute. This won't take long. The water's still fairly hot; I had some not too long ago." She pried up a lid of a large wood-burning range and began making up a fire, over which she slammed down a heavy iron kettle.

He could see very little detail of the candlelit kitchen. The cabinets and furnishings were dark and old-fashioned. The stovepipe was flued into a wide fireplace, which had been bricked up and painted over. The walls were occupied by a weird assembly of graffiti, banners,

11

and collages, which seemed to be cut from snips of cloth or colored paper. The only things in the room that had anything at all to do with the everyday world were a checkered sack of dried catfood and a carton of milk powder. The wide windows and back screen door stood open to the warm air of the September-rich night, but indoors a flavor of woodsmoke and ancient cooking grease hung over everything.

"How many people live here with you?" he asked.

"No one. Only me. And the cats."

"*Cats*?" Martin frowned. Still this house didn't have the ammoniac stench of the home of a crazy little cat woman.

"Yes. I have four cats and four kittens. They're great company. Most of them are out hunting right now, though, except Trilby." Trilby stared from a box on the floor, which she shared with the kittens. "Sit down now. You'll be better after a while. I promise you will."

Her voice was quick and gentle, soft and chattering. It coaxed him into obedience. He drew up a heavy oak chair to a round claw-legged table. Another cat galloped in and sprang up on his knees. He started to lift it down, but it leaned its warm furry body against him trustingly and he dropped his hands to his sides and slumped on the chair, with nothing to say and confusion gathering in his mind.

"That's Brandenburg," the girl said. "Don't pay any attention to him; he's fool enough to love everybody. Even my mother." She sat down calmly and waited quietly for the kettle to boil. Presently it began steaming and rattling. She rose, reached into a mason jar that stood near the sink, and thrust a handful of leaves into a big brown teapot. Then she caught up the iron kettle barehanded. She was evidently not as fragile as she looked. A sharp pungent fragrance arose as she brewed the tea and collected cups and saucers. "I was smart to keep extras of

12

everything. Here. Doesn't that smell good? Doesn't it make you feel better?"

He tried to drink, but set the cup down. "I can't swallow this."

"You're not supposed to. Take a deep breath of the steam. Or at least pretend to. Let it sort of waft over you. We all have to do it that way. It's so aromatic and good. At least, it's a lot better than nothing. Try."

He bent his head again over the tea and decided that he was too shaken up to drink it. "What do you mean by all of you? First you said no one else—I thought all along this must be some sort of commune."

"Well, I was all alone, but I guess I'm not any more. I haven't told you my name. It's Ashgrove Frazier. As in the grove of Ashtaroth. Or amid the dark shades of the lonely ash grove. Please tell me yours."

"Martin. Evans."

"Martin, I really don't know how to explain this. . ."

He stood up. The cat ran off. "Thanks for all you've done, but I've got my breath now."

"No." The girl stood up too, as if to restrain him.

"I need to report this before it gets any later. Can you tell me the shortest way to a phone? You must understand I don't know this country at all, and I can't move my car."

"I wouldn't worry about it. You don't need it."

Martin curbed his temper. "Lady, someone I don't even know is lying down there on the road, and I will probably wind up either in jail for manslaughter or in the nut ward because I still don't remember anything about what happened."

"That is *you*. Rather, it's your body. You are dead. You're a ghost. So am I. I really hate this. It's brutal. I thought when you found out you couldn't drink the tea you'd understand what had happened. I don't like this. I never broke this kind of news to anyone before, or saw anyone who had been killed. But if you don't believe me, go down to the road and look again."

"Oh, God."

"I'm an atheist, myself, but if you care to phrase it that way . . ."

Martin turned and banged out of the kitchen. When after a few minutes he had not come back, Ashgrove went after him, down to the road.

"I have a concussion. I'm hallucinating. And I don't understand why you won't tell me the way to a telephone."

"Martin, you really cannot stay down here like this. It won't do you one bit of good. Please come back up to the house, and we can really talk. Someone driving by will report the accident as soon as it's daybreak, and the rescue squad will come from Masonborough."

"You're trying to tell me that isn't a hitchhiker. It's me and I'm dead."

"No, this is you. But you're dead."

"I really must be concussion-drunk out of my mind. I'm seeing double. I don't understand why I don't pass out." He mentally reviewed his address, phone number, birthday, and army serial number. He must get hold of himself. It was not like him to talk so much to strangers. "This is the day after Labor Day . . . Tuesday morning . . . and I'm somewhere between Richmond and Washington. I left Raleigh sometime after midnight, and I'm almost home. If I can remember all that, I must not have a concussion. Something else must be wrong."

"Something else *is*. Listen, Martin—"

"One of us is crazy. In either case, I think I'd better leave."

14

"What is it going to take? What is it going to take? Look—his hair is the same as yours. He's your size. You're wearing his clothes. And don't ask me why that is; maybe we get the clothes we deserve; I always adored this sweater of mine, but that's a whole other story. That one lying yonder—he's meat and bone, and you're not, any more. Neither am I. Listen. Would you believe I've been dead for two years?"

"Stoned out of your gourd for two years, maybe."

"Come back to the house. I'll put my hand in the fire for you."

"I'm in enough trouble. I don't need atrocity charges."

She tucked in one corner of her mouth and threw out her hands, seeming exasperated. "I know I'm not explaining this very well. I spend too much time by myself. Conversation is strange to me. Maybe when the real people get here, you'll understand better. It's only a short time till day. Stay here with me. Don't go off looking for people. You'll just scare them silly. Believe me, I know. Then, if someone doesn't come pretty soon, I'll help you get wherever you want to go. Come away from here, I don't like this. You think that I'm some sort of lunatic, but I'm really not. I'm really dead. This is my house that I haunt." Even in his fatigue and despair he noticed that her strong Virginia accent turned *house* into *hoose*. "But you can stay in it as long as you want to."

Martin swayed on his feet. He remembered that he had not slept the night before and had been driving for several hours without a break. He felt even more exhausted and lightheaded than the circumstances called for. All sense of what time it might be had left him. Still, he wondered if the girl might not have some relative or even a nurse nearby who might help him. If the house wasn't a commune, maybe it was a private asylum. In any case, he wanted to get away from the wreck, and sit down and think consecutively.

He went with her again, through the overgrown garden and up to the wide front steps of the house. She sat on the top and he sat on the bottom. Honeysuckle—he had not known it still bloomed so late in the year—climbed all through the dark shrubbery by the steps. She picked a sprig and smelled of it gratefully.

Then she said gently, "Tell me something about what happened. What went wrong? Where were you going from, to?"

It was not the time for anyone to come on like a Southern lady, asking little sociable questions. But he needed to talk anyway. All his past life began to seem to him, not great exactly, but delightful, beloved, and innocent in a way he could not readily describe. He longed to get back into it as one might long to escape into a favorite familiar story. Telling the girl about it might make it seem real.

"I don't know what went wrong. Right now I live in the District—Washington, I mean."

"I know what the District is," she said with some sharpness.

"Well, I live in the District"—the repetition made him feel better—"but I was coming from Raleigh. I worked Memorial Day, so I had off Labor Day. I had been down to Raleigh to see a girl over the weekend. And even though I waited so late to leave, the traffic was incredible. You couldn't even get on the Petersburg Turnpike. It's the armpit of the northeast corridor. . . . Excuse me."

"Someone once told me 'armpit' was a euphemism."

Martin let this comment go right by. He was still trying to order his story. The predawn chill struck cold on him. He leaned his elbows on his knees and grasped his

16

forehead in stone-cold hands. "So I decided there was no point in even going near Richmond. That's where I made my big mistake, I guess. I crossed the James River somewhere upstream, but there were so many other rivers and not very many north-south roads, and I came even more out of my way than I meant to. I was counting on my sense of direction, and I thought I could make good time on the back roads; less traffic, anyway. Well, so I was going to come up through Warrenton or Manassas. But I didn't get nearly that far."

"No. Not nearly."

"And I got onto your road here—it's amazing what they'll put a number on in Virginia, and call it a road—and I went too fast, or something went wrong with the car; I don't know." He stopped short. The idea of the dead man who undoubtedly looked like him, lying face down by the road, was taking up too much of his mind.

"Didn't you have a map?"

"Of Virginia? I usually just drive through on the Eighty-five–Ninety-five. Who needs a map of Virginia, for God's sake?"

"As it turned out, you did," the girl said astringently.

You have to watch these Southern ladies, Martin thought. I really walked into that one. "I reckon you're right," he said with weary courtesy.

She moved down a step and began to rub his back. "Does that make you feel any better at all?"

Her hands were as cold as his own.

He said, "Tell me honestly, how do you get away with living here? Doesn't anyone give you trouble or try to run you off?"

"Well, thus far they haven't. It's really morally my house. Morally. My grandfather left it to me, because he didn't get along with my mother. She was no blood kin to him anyway. My father disappeared some time ago. I don't even remember him. But that's a whole other story. When I died, I didn't leave a will—I never thought to. Probably the house went to my mother. I imagine she's having trouble getting her title clear, or something. My grandfather Frazier wanted me to have it, not her. Well, Francie Lee—that's my mother—put everything of value in storage and took off for greener pastures. New Orleans, maybe. I don't know."

His attention suddenly seized on one phrase. "What do you mean, you didn't leave a will?"

"Well, I wasn't really expecting I'd die. It was a foolish mistake. We all make foolish mistakes, but some are more fatal than others. I don't like to talk about it. I'll tell you sometime maybe, but not now. Why don't you stay here awhile? I like being alone—I have great fun—but it might be comforting to have company. I haven't met terribly many ghosts. The ones I have met are awful, but you don't seem to be. At first glance," she added.

Martin shouted, "Damn it, you're trying to make me as crazy as you are." He snatched her around to face him.

She looked back at him steadily and said, "I guess I talked too much, too soon."

They both stood up. He grasped her hands. They were small, thin, and light, smelling faintly of clean earth. And quite cold. He touched her cheek and it was cold. Dawn was washing the sky clear. Great leafy silhouettes of trees piled up against it and sleepy mockingbirds chattered. Away to the west, across the fields, the horn of a diesel locomotive blew.

He was very much aware that he had been up all night and that there was a ruinous day in front of him. But curiously his strength was gathering again.

He said, "It's getting daylight."

She said, "But there where western glooms are gathering, The dark will end the dark, if anything."

That was her most unnerving remark yet. He said, "Enough. I'm leaving."

"Where to?"

"Into town, wherever that is. Anywhere there's people and someone to tell me I'm not out of my mind. They can put me in jail, arrest me for drugs, murder—you name it. Fine. There must be someone who won't talk riddles and scare me to death."

He broke off and ran down the lane. At the road where the wreck lay, he turned left, which was roughly north, not looking behind him.

Ashgrove stood still, her face set unhappily and her hands clenched on nothing. "I guess nobody else can go there for him," she said. Then, raising her voice, she called, "Don't forget the way back!" But she could not tell if Martin heard.

The other cats were coming in—Pyracantha and Tom Scarborough. Tom was large, black and white, and sinister looking. Pyracantha was a nervous calico, brindled in earth colors. Brandenburg joined them. He was the color of golden oak, with some Persian fluffing out his ruff and tail. They were all strays that at one time or another had wandered up to the Frazier place or been abandoned by the road. Hunters or not, they were all hungry now. They hunched and stretched and quivered around Ashgrove's legs.

"All right, come on," she said to them. They convoyed her from the front of the house to the back, where she rattled food into their bowls and mixed up milk. The mother cat Trilby hopped out of her box, stalked over, and harassed the others until they let her eat first.

"Another dreadful day of fear and toil had come to Mordor," Ashgrove said happily. She stepped out to smell the scents of the warming world and admire the late colors of her back garden.

It did look as though it might be a rather dreadful day. Everything was baked with weeks of drought. The sky closed in tightly, but no rain fell. She frowned upward. Things were not likely to change that day. Still, as long as her well held out, she would do all right and keep her plants flourishing. The scarlet sage, petunias, and marigolds had done well all summer; so had the perennial potherbs, the geraniums, and the other tender things in pots. Back here she had both space and privacy and was free to garden as best she might.

The front of the house was smothered in maple shade, and down on the south slope stood a grove of hickories, but here at the back stood a solitary tulip poplar, immensely tall and far older than the house. Leaves from it dropped onto the flower beds and clay pots—leaves that were yellow, white-spotted in places. She frowned again. The tree had a disease that she thought was called anthracnose. It had probably been infected by the sycamore tree down by the road. There was little she could do for it; some years were worse than others. The drought this summer had been hard on it.

If not for that sycamore tree, which her grandfather had defended against all comers, including the Commonwealth of Virginia, the impossibly sharp S-bend would have been graded out of the road, and that young man named Martin would have got safely to Manassas, or wherever he was going.

Where was he going now? What would become of him?

Anything might, Ashgrove thought. She was not laying any bets. He did not look predictable at all. He was one of those people who look serious and scholarly but do not necessarily turn out to be either. Nor did he look as though he exactly belonged with his feet under her kitchen table.

I did everything for him that I could, but maybe I didn't go about it the right way.

Wonder if he'll ever find his way back here, if I'll ever see him again.

Is there anything else I ought to be doing?

She unsuccessfully tried to put away the thought of the wreck.

If he ever does get back, there may be something down there that he would want.

Down at the road again, she winced, wishing that she had something to put over the dead. She couldn't keep the ants from crawling on him, but at least she didn't want to watch them. On the driver's side of the wrecked car, the safety belt dangled loose and useless. But in the back there lay an old duffel bag and a neatly cased musical instrument, both soundly strapped in. Stuffed in around them was an old army blanket.

"Mm," Ashgrove said in dismay and irritation. She unstrapped the musical instrument—which turned out to be a guitar—and tried to leave the back looking as though it had been undisturbed. Still she felt no guilt. Guilt was not a thing that she often felt. Martin, desperately unhappy and upset as he was, would need that guitar, and she was going to keep it for him.

Then she took the army blanket and grimly laid it over the body. The rescue squad would wonder whose work that was. Let them. They'd never find out.

She carried the guitar back to the kitchen and opened its case. It was beautifully made and seemed unhurt. She could not tell whether it had been knocked out of tune. She swept her hand across the strings. They spoke quietly in an open chord that told her nothing. The fragrance of aromatic wood drifted through the sound hole.

She set the guitar in a far corner of the kitchen, away from the heat of the stove. Still she was nervous. She could not rest, nor could she amuse herself. That was unusual. She had been doing one or the other for two years.

I wish someone would come. I wish someone would come. I can't sit here forever waiting, can I? Did I need this?

No. Nobody needed it.

She gave the teacups and saucers a bachelor's wash under the pitcher-pump, which stood in the breezeway between the kitchen and the main house. Then she fetched a worn pencil and the cheap ledger in which she kept garden observations.

Dear Jake (she wrote),

Something rather out of the ordinary has happened and I can't do anything about it, and you're the only one I can tell. Please call the patrol and the rescue squad. There was a wreck out by my place early this morning before daybreak, and someone was killed—almost instantly, it looked like. That isn't the strangest part. He stood up from the body—his ghost did—it was rather like in the Ancient Mariner, if you know what I mean—and he couldn't believe what had happened, and he's gone raging off to town, and I just don't know what will happen now. So if you hear any weird rumors, you'll understand, but please report the wreck, because it's worrying me out of my mind.

Love.

She tore the page from the ledger without signing her name.

To get to where Jake lived, you could go up by the road or across the fields. Ashgrove chose the fields, for many of them belonged to her, or at least she claimed them. They had been part of the old Frazier acreage when her grandfather had lived and farmed there, and before that too. She passed through a gap in the thick privet hedge that enclosed the backyard on three sides and screened the barns and shed from the house. North and west of the house lay the orchard, which she and her grandfather had both loved. The early apples were in. She picked up one that had fallen, to carry to Jake along with the note. The apple had not been sprayed and was small and speckled, though it would still taste good and tart. The orchard was suffering; every year a blight spread farther upon it from the encroaching cedars, and the old trees would nearly defoliate in a desperate effort to give strength to their fruit.

Before his death, her grandfather had made hardly any profit on the orchard, but he still loved it; it had been planted by his own grandfather in memory of destroyed orchards back in the Shenandoah Valley. After that war, many Virginians went west, but the Fraziers were different and moved east, and east they had stayed.

Beyond the orchard lay the old fields and pastures, going now to pale broomstraw and dark cedars, and gay with joe-pye weed, Queen Anne's lace, and the tall wild asters and goldenrod of late summer. Ashgrove took to a narrow track that ran between these fields and skirted the woods—rough ruts in the gingerbread-russet earth made years ago by wagons and kept open by tractors. This was Piedmont country. It rolled gently west from the fall line, cut by the small rivers with their Indian, English, and dog-Latin names, away toward the misty granite spine of the Blue Ridge.

Ashgrove walked barefoot and tireless, though in places

23

the track was as rocky as an old stream bed. She went barefoot in all weathers, but her neat narrow feet were never stubbed or calloused, and for all her diggings in the dirt her hands never became soiled or rough. Her high-school gym teacher had told her that she had no kinesthetic sense. Her mother had nagged her to watch her posture and not stand so slump-shouldered. Ashgrove stubbornly wandered on, keeping her eyes open and not worrying how she held her shoulders or where she put her feet.

Here ran the main-line railroad in a double right-of-way, built on an embankment. The field track climbed abruptly to a grade crossing marked by a worn crossbuck, and then dipped down again, turning north to follow the rails. Ashgrove hated this place and always had, even though it was called by her name and had been known as Frazier's Crossing since the more opulent days when apples had been shipped from it and trains had stopped there to load them on. The apple-packing shed was still standing, half derelict. It was not for this ruin that she hated it. There was some other reason. She had never known exactly what. Her grandfather had never told her of anything that would explain the feeling. Her guess was that something ugly and violent had happened here once. It would be a dangerous place for a wreck. Someone's old Model T might have stalled going up that grade, its wheels caught over the rails, the locomotive bearing down, the whistle screaming, the brakes gasping, the wheels scattering sparks into the night. She flinched.

You have the worst ideas. I don't know what gets into you.

She picked up her heels and began to run. Jake's place was not much farther now, up on the county road that crossed the old back road to Masonborough.

WATERLOO HIGH SCHOOL LIBRARY
1464 INDUSTRY RD.
ATWATER, OHIO 44201

24

Jake Galey was one of Ashgrove's oldest friends. For that reason, or for some other, he seemed to be the only living soul who was now able to see her. She said she had known him forever, though that was not true. He had come from someplace in the Midwest. For a while he had taught English in the Mason County High School, and she had been one of his students. He told her that she was one of the most enthusiastic people he had ever known, and one of the worst writers. She loved him dearly anyway, for she found his unsparing irony salutary, in small doses.

After a few frustrating years of teaching, Jake had decided to do something completely different, more in the Renaissance-man line. He bought a country store and filling station that came up for sale, claiming that he wanted to be his own boss and could make more money this way. Evidently he did, too. Ashgrove suspected him of being engaged on a book, probably about Mason County and its denizens. He said that if that were true, she would be the last to know, since she had not read any significant modern prose since *The Lord of the Rings* hit the newsstands.

Ashgrove, after her short life had so suddenly and surprisingly been ended, had found herself wandering out of Mason County Memorial Hospital and down the back roads toward her home, which would be empty as soon as her mother could finish packing. Being a ghost did not come hard. Having fitted poorly into her skinny body, she had always half wanted to be a ghost anyway, and she seemed to be still running on adrenaline, or on something else that wouldn't quit. A great stroke of one-upsmanship had come to her, her first social act in her new state. She had climbed the outside stairs to where Jake Galey lived in two rooms over his store with his worldliest possession, a stupendous hi-fi rig, which was then going full belt with the Verdi *Requiem*.

When he finally answered her knock, she announced, "I'm Catherine Earnshaw; I'm come home."

Nothing fazed Jake. He told her she needed a good spanking, but he wasn't going to give it to her. Then he took another look.

"Ha," Ashgrove said delightedly. "I came to tell you you'd better switch to low-lead white lightning."

"Come in and listen and shut up," Jake replied.

Unlike most people, he had no deep-rooted objection to ghosts. He once said he'd rather see than be one. His mind was open to odd quirks of experience. If the ghost couldn't be anyone like Dostoevski or Mozart, Ashgrove would do well enough; at least she spoke English. They set up a cock-eyed symbiosis. She placidly haunted her house, he ran his store. What little she needed from it, such as catfood or an occasional seed packet, he let her have. She cooked and cleaned for him sometimes, but usually he preferred his own housekeeping. They read each other's books and laughed at each other's jokes. His cooking grease went into her homemade candles. None of his customers had ever guessed that he had made a friend of a female ghost, underaged and undersized. It was Ashgrove's scrupulous practice to visit him infrequently and at very odd hours.

This time she did not expect him to be up yet, or if he was, he would be busy. She planned to leave the apple and the note at the door of his upstairs quarters. But as she started up she met him coming down, carrying a couple of swollen sacks of garbage. He was a burly, barrel-chested man in his early thirties, with shaggy tan hair and beard, who looked as if he should be carrying something more dramatic than garbage—a Viking ax, possibly.

26

She said, "Hail, Caesar."

He said, "Hail, yes."

"I didn't want to bother you. I just brought you this note."

"Who from?"

"Me."

He dumped down the garbage, wiped his hands on his grubby work pants, accepted the apple, and read the note, while Ashgrove fidgeted.

"Ancient Mariner, hm."

"Well, that part may have been an exaggeration."

"I told you to watch that, Ashgrove. If this is a joke, it isn't very funny."

"It isn't funny at all. Nor is it a joke."

"How many were there? Just one?"

"Yes."

"You're sure he's dead and not just unconscious."

"Oh, yes. Oh, yes. It was very distressing. I don't want to talk about it."

"I've never known you not to want to talk about anything."

"Times are changing. Well. He didn't understand me. He didn't take my word. He went off looking for the way to town, and other people. I have no idea where he is or what will happen—I hope nothing awful—but he's another one like me. Or sort of," she added.

"All right, you get in the car and I'll run you over there and take a look."

"Thanks." Ashgrove did not want to go by Frazier's Crossing again anyway. Once a day was enough. She began to ask Jake a question, but he went on:

"If we meet anyone, or get stopped by any troopers, you've got to promise not to embarrass me."

"You know I wouldn't. You know me better than that."

27

"Otherwise, I won't mess with giving you any more grease."

"For behold, darkness shall cover the earth, and gross darkness the people."

"You're the only Bible-quoting atheist I ever met."

"Can't help it. It's my upbringing. I used to read the Bible and the hymnbook in church instead of listening to the service. Anyway, that isn't really the Bible; it's the *Messiah*."

"Let's go. If anybody asks, I'll say I'm going fishing. It's still early."

Jake drove an ancient, battered car of Swedish make whose odometer had already turned over—he claimed only once. They chugged down the county road, running between more scrubby fields of broomstraw and cedar, and turned onto the narrow lane-and-a-half that ran in front of Ashgrove's house. This road ran north to Masonborough and south, eventually, to Richmond. They met no one on it. The scene of the wreck was unchanged.

Jake said, "Mm. Look at that. No skid marks. He must've been sound asleep." He knelt down and turned back the army blanket partway. "Well. We've got to get him up out of here. What was he, your age?"

"Older, I think."

"Well," Jake said again, getting to his feet. "I'll drive back and phone the squad. Will you be all right?"

"Yes. Why not?"

"I guess you will. Take care."

"Thanks," she said absently. She walked back to the house and sat down on the kitchen steps, not waiting to watch Jake leave. Presently she heard the sounds of sirens coming from Masonborough, and heavy engines grinding to a halt down on her road. Not till they were gone did she rise. She went up to the front room of her house, where the old Chickering upright still stood, and pressed her weightless fingers into the jangling yellow keys.

# 2

MARTIN, DRIVEN BY ANGER AND ALARM, started off at a run
up Ashgrove's road, which crossed another road after a
few hundred yards. If he had turned left, which was west,
he would soon have reached the railroad and Jake Galey's
store; if he had kept going west he would have eventually
reached the federal highway and been back on the right
track to Washington. Not knowing this country, he
studied the sign at the intersection. The town of Masonborough was apparently five miles up the road, in the
direction he was already going.

Someone else was heading into Masonborough early,
driving an old Chevrolet. Martin began walking backward
down the middle of the road, signaling it to stop. It came
on at forty miles an hour, its headlights still glowing

dimly. "Stop!" Martin yelled. The driver pushed a hand across his eyes and switched up his brights, slowing down a little. Then the brights went down again and the car speeded up and passed on. Martin jumped aside, but the wind of its passage barely ruffled him. "Bastard," he said. "Goddamn." He had never felt so alone.

He did not understand what was keeping him from dropping in his tracks. He felt half stupefied, half intensified, as though he had taken a heavy dose of strong painkiller. He was not hurting, but his nerves were jangling, and still a strange calm possessed him. After a second and third and fourth driver had shot by him, he quit signaling.

I've heard of not getting involved, but this is preposterous.

He set one foot in front of another, not even looking up as cars passed him with slightly more frequency. He passed a dead possum lying in the road, an unearthly grin at one end, innards spilling out at the other.

Possums are not the brightest.

The light was growing, but there would be no sun that day, only a silverish splotch in the sky. The country seemed drained of color, like the background in a dream, when the dreamer thinks he is dreaming in color and cannot understand why everything looks wrong. It was oddly desolate. This back road to Masonborough bordered few farmed fields or dwelling-houses. All he saw was oak woods, looking rusty around the edges; fields of pale grass; and cedars, many of them, shaped like the ace of spades and nearly as black, lining the fences and shouldering out into the road. It was going to be smotheringly hot, but Martin did not feel smothered.

He came to a place where someone had rather obviously run over or otherwise annoyed a skunk. Then he came to a

31

trailer development, which looked like a clutch of abandoned boxcars. It was still early. He wondered if it was too early to ask for the use of a phone. But his watch was not on his wrist.

That bothered him, but it was the least of his worries. He thought the strap might have broken during the wreck, about which he could still remember little or nothing.

Somewhere in the trailer camp several dogs began to yap lamentably. Martin did not feel like fighting dogs, or dealing with angry owners. He moved on.

Here was a filling station, grimy white stucco. It was closed at this hour, but it had an outside pay phone. He could call the police from here. The number was listed in the front of the directory—a meager and tattered object. This phone was not designed for a real emergency. You still had to have a dime to get the operator. He reached in his pocket for change and found nothing. Nothing in any of his pockets. His clothes felt thin and sleazy on him, and he felt thin and wispy under the clothes.

"Don't ask me why that is. Maybe we get the clothes we deserve," said an earnest, breathless voice in his mind. "Would you believe I've been dead for two years?"

He decided to walk till he collapsed or met someone rational, whichever came first.

He did not collapse before he reached town. Nor did he meet anyone walking; the only people who were out were driving. Masonborough grew up around him in the usual manner of small towns, putting its ugliest side foremost. There were the expected cracker-box developments, discount shopping centers, hamburger places, and filling stations. The lane-and-a-half country road widened to a strip, which in its turn gave way to a broad, oak-shaded street. The oldest part of Masonborough had been built for spaciousness and comfort, and in a more crowded, less comfortable age, it had kept as much the same as it could.

Many of the large old houses were offices now, but not the office that Martin was after. He meant to go straight to the law and get the agony over.

Straight ahead was what looked to be a courthouse square. The sheriff's office will most likely be there, he thought, with so little dread that it surprised him. By this time he felt that he would welcome the arrival of some iron-jawed, iron-gutted sheriff telling him that he was in a heap of trouble.

I'll say, you don't know the half.

The courthouse was a little fortress of gray granite. Up on a pedestal in the shady square, the requisite Confederate soldier leaned on his rifle. For some inarticulate reason, Martin saluted him.

Around a corner he found a sign directing him to the sheriff's office, which was not open now, and would not be till nine o'clock.

What now?

The Masonborough city hall was in an old office building across from the courthouse. A door was unlocked beside a sign that read "Police." This time his luck was in, or at least the police were. A sleepy-looking officer was there behind the desk, but did not look up as Martin stepped in from the cigar-smelling hall.

"I want to report a fatal accident. It happened several hours ago, but it's taken me all this time to get here."

They would question him closely about that. Fine.

The clock on the wall said half past seven, and the mockingbirds and jays in the trees of the square were yelling their heads off.

"Excuse me. Didn't you hear me? This is important. Someone has been killed, and it was probably my fault."

The policeman said, "It's too early in the morning." He rubbed his eyes, stretched, and stood up.

Desperation took hold of Martin then. He bolted around behind the desk and seized the other man by the shoulders. "Goddamn it, lock me up, I don't care; just pay me some mind. I haven't talked to anybody but myself and dead men and crazy women since I left Raleigh. Make me feel like I exist for a change."

The man winced and shuddered, easily shaking off Martin's grasp. He was no more than a boy, younger and slighter than Martin. "I've really got the jumps. I'm just not awake good. Frank! Have you got any coffee in there?"

"Okay, Roy. Be ready in a minute," Frank shouted from the inner office.

Martin doubled his fists and yelled several of the most virulent curses that his varied career had taught him.

Nothing happened. No platoon of armed men stormed in and overpowered him. Frank said that the coffee was done, and Roy went in to get some. Martin slapped his right hand on the wall with all the strength he had. He felt the impact lightly, but it made no sound and did not hurt him. However, a large map hanging on the wall began to sway gently.

"Come back to my house and I'll put my hand in the fire for you," pleaded a voice in his mind.

I'm in enough trouble, he told her again.

Among the other clutter on the desk was a book of matches. He struck one and held it to his sleeve, which refused to catch. He set his jaw and held the match to the back of his other hand. The little flame burned serenely, igniting nothing and causing no pain. He let the match burn away in his fingers and lit the whole book at once. It blazed away painlessly with a strong odor of sulfur. The advice to finish your education charred to nothing.

Roy came back in and said, "Jesus Christ."

Martin closed his fist around the blaze and extinguished it. He said, "I should never have done that."

Frank called, "What?"

"Nothing," Roy answered in a controlled voice.

The map on the wall was still quivering a little, though the room was otherwise dead still. Ashes sifted onto the desk.

"I'm sorry," Martin said, though he was sure now that they could neither see nor hear him. He left the police station hastily and stood on the sidewalk wondering where to go next.

The courthouse square seemed as good as any other place. At least it offered breathing room. Or probably elbow room was a more accurate phrase. He wondered, if anyone were to bump into him on the street, what that person would say or do. He did not want to find out, at least not at the moment.

The town of Masonborough was slowly opening up to the new day, such as it was. In front of the grocery store a man was sweeping the sidewalk. People were heading into the Merchants' Café, breakfast bound. Eggs and bacon lay heavy on the air. Martin turned away.

There was still not much traffic, but he looked before he crossed the street anyway, for his old reflexes were still with him. He sat down on a bench. Then he lay down on it. It was too short, and he had to draw his heels up under him. Then he decided that lying in the grass was better anyway. He stretched out under one of the large oaks of the square. The grass was poor; shade of the trees and summer drought had not helped it. It was not uncomfortable, though. Martin stared up at the heavy grayish sky through the multiple scallops of the oak leaves.

Score one to the girl who claimed she haunted that old house. She had tried to help him without being too pressing, done about everything but throw him down and sit on him. He believed her now; he was really dead, even though that was not the most incredible part. He had long known—or at least entertained the notion—that he was someday going to die. At certain times, as when traveling in airplanes, he knew that he might die quite soon. And always he feared dying worse than he feared death, for dying would most likely hurt, but death was nothingness and would feel like nothing.

Score minus two for him. He had been wrong on both counts. Dying was what had felt like nothing.

He felt obscurely cheated. As well as his life, he had lost his death. When you died, you ought to know it, even though at the same time you hoped that you wouldn't; he had always left his safety belt off from fear of being trapped sometime and burned alive. But he still could not remember how the wreck had happened. He had been a fool to get sucked off into the mazes of the backcountry, steering for the Dipper, faded and far-flung, whenever he could. He had also been a little drunk, something he had not admitted to the girl. But not that drunk. He had been counting on the constant swing-and-jostle of driving on poorly graded and surfaced roads to keep him awake.

Evidently it hadn't worked.

I've been run through a strainer.

Put through a keyhole.

Dragged through a hedge ass-backward.

And something is still left of me, though I don't know exactly what.

That was the most incredible part.

Still flat on his back, he held his mouth in a tongue-tied position and said experimentally, "Six monce ago I couldn't even spell ghost, and now I are one." But the skit fell flat.

Any minute now, I'll wake up in a hospital bed, and the nurses will come running, yelling, "He's out of his coma!"

Being a ghost just isn't the sort of thing that happens to me. I don't believe in ghosts; I never even believed in the alleged immortal soul, the resurrection of the body, and the life everlasting. And I wasn't done living.

Martin was accustomed to go through life as best he could, frequently saying, "Oh, God," and occasionally, "Who dealt this mess?" but never receiving much of a reply, nor expecting one. He got no comment now.

He turned on his face, there in the poor scrubby grass, and lay there for a time; how long, he never exactly knew. Ants walked up his arm, over the bridge of his nose, and around the curve of his eye socket, never disturbing him at all.

Presently he decided that lying there was really not much better than being dead and buried, and that it might be wise to try something else.

Mainly, being a ghost was cold. There was a dull chill on him, like the first grip of fever, but with none of fever's listlessness. He could hardly help noticing things, whether he wanted to or not. There was the Confederate soldier still, seen from a different angle now. Half a dozen squirrels ran to and fro, squabbling over acorns and adding their angry little voices to those of the chattering birds.

Surely not too many people could have had this experience before.

"Except me," said the girl's voice.

"Be quiet," Martin said, half angrily.

Ghosts. Henrik Ibsen. Great Caesar's Ghost. Abraham Lincoln walks at night. Anne Boleyn with her head tucked underneath her arm. The headless brakeman—where had he heard that story?—swinging his lantern. The beautiful girl hitchhiking in an evening dress, trying to get home. Someone draped in a hollow-eyed Halloween sheet. What had he in common with any of them?

He looked down at his hands. They were long and lanky like the rest of him, with the usual accumulation of scars, calluses, and prominent tendons—the same as before and yet subtly changed, in the way they caught, or did not catch, the light. He still wore his Levi's and chambray shirt, old comfortable clothes. He looked just the same as ever, as far as he could tell. There was still no sun. He could not see if he threw a shadow.

I will just have to wait until Groundhog Day, I reckon.

A squirrel darted up and looked at him, or seemed to. It had foolish beady eyes and a foolish fat stomach. He said, "Go away. It isn't Groundhog Day yet." It darted off again, tail twitching frenetically.

Well, I can't stay here in the courthouse square and talk to the damn squirrels forever.

Where can I go then?

Not only can nobody see me, but they can see whatever I might handle. That's beautiful.

He had not been particularly amused by the incident in the police station. What good had it done? None. Taken ten years off the guy's life, probably.

For all his skepticism and stubbornness, Martin had developed an odd courtesy, a respect for other people's emotional territory as well as a desire to protect his own. He had not lost these qualities; indeed they had strengthened. In his anomalous position, maybe no one could help him, but he would use it to hurt no one.

A strong memory came back to him, of a narrative he had once read, written by a prominent author. This man's son had killed himself and then allegedly striven to reach his family and friends with the crazed antics of a poltergeist. The story had been widely publicized—Martin had read it in a popular magazine—but everything about it had repelled him, and still did. None of that for him. He was not going to be found singeing off anyone's hair or scaring people up the wall.

His family would have to do without him, just as he would have to do without them.

The girl in Raleigh—Jean was her name—would have to do without him too.

Right now, it was not Jeannie but his mother that he thought of most vividly, a little, spare, wiry lady who had raised four boys, Martin being third, and practically never lost her sense of humor the whole time. In fact, maybe that was a defense as well as a response. She was always joking, but she didn't really tell you much. His family were not articulate people. They were not letter writers, either. After he had left home, he had not kept close touch with them, but he at least knew that they were there.

They were still there. He was the one who wasn't.

It was true that some people could see ghosts, or claimed they could. Suppose someone he knew turned out to be one of these? Which would be worse: to be seen or not to be seen? He wasn't going home to find out.

What the hell happened to you, Martin? You're a shadow of your former self.

No way.

All the ghosts he had ever heard of wanted to go home, but he would be different.

Forgetting about Jeannie would be still another story. Not to forget her would probably be worse. He had met her at the beach the summer before. She was studying nursing in Raleigh now, at one of the hospitals there. She was a strong little person, even-tempered and matter-of-fact. But she wasn't that strong. She would be sorry. But she didn't need to be horrified with it.

Most likely the only people who could see him now were frightful unwashed women named Madame Anna or Sister Faith, with soiled turbans and tarnished earrings.

"And me," came from the voice that kept interrupting him, in a tone of astringent patience.

At least the girl had looked clean.

He shook off the thought of her and considered again.

He was not going back to either of those cities that he had lately called home—Washington or Baltimore. The familiar streets would have no place for him now. The apartment house where he had last lived was bad enough without getting a name for being haunted. Washington did not need any more haunted houses, nor houses with things wrong with them.

He wondered sardonically how long it might be before his roommates noticed that he was gone.

It was time, then, to start from where he was right now, with this left-handed gift of ghosthood. Gift? No one had given it. It was an accident, the convergence of circumstances: late hours, lack of sleep, a little too much to drink, and a bad place in the road. The oddest things turned out to be capital crimes.

Where he was right now, this Masonborough, was just a small town in Virginia, neither here nor there, too far from Richmond, too far from Washington to be part of anywhere much. He had hardly even noticed it on the maps. Yet he might have guessed what it would be like. He had seen this square in the movies and on the evening news. The First Presbyterian Church faced the First Baptist Church, but the Presbyterians had been there about seventy-five years longer than the Baptists. The

Episcopal Church was smaller and older than either, and stood down a side street. A few gracefully built old offices were interspersed with gingerbread Gothic stores, their eaves dripping with carving. Across from the city hall stood an antiquated, balconied hotel. Then there was the First Bank of Mason County. A four-sided clock jutted from its side, but it was evidently in disrepair; the hands were missing. Past the Episcopal church a shiny green-and-white sign pointed the way to the hospital.

If it were not for this sleek modern sign, the automobile traffic that thickened around the square, and the gas-station sign that hung beyond the hotel, blocking the trees, you might well question what century you were in.

What could there be here that he wanted; what was there for him to do with himself? Yes, there was something, or there had better be. He wanted his guitar. He had taken it with him to Raleigh, as he took it almost everywhere. Unless it was actually under his hand, he always feared that it might get ripped off, and even if he could get together enough money, he would never find another one that he liked as well.

It was unlikely that he would ever again have to worry about money.

What did they do with people's personal things? They took them to the same place they took your body—the morgue, probably.

*That* was a thought. Unpleasant, but a thought.

Where is the morgue in a town the size of this? Probably at the hospital.

You just had to go by the probabilities.

Even if nothing else in the world was left to him, he meant to have his guitar. He set off down the shady streets of Masonborough, away from the power of the law and of everything else, appallingly limited, and appallingly free.

It was not a long walk to the hospital, and he still was not tired—not properly tired. He would almost have welcomed a feeling of real tiredness rather than this spaced-out sensation.

By the time he reached the hospital his nervousness was worse than ever. Each time he met or passed someone, he felt like some derelict figure of scandal or a man with an ugly handicap. He was tired of people looking at him— not quite looking at him—looking through him—wincing and flinching, frowning as though something had come between them and the daylight. He thought again of the stone soldier and the squirrels. He was one and they were the others; he watched from his point of vantage while they ran about on errands that absorbed them intensely but which they would soon forget. Yet he did not wish other people any ill or offense. Why intrude himself on them, becoming a horror show? Or a side show, depending on how you looked at it. He ought to keep moving.

Blending into the landscape was one thing, but this was something else. He thought he might whistle a verse of some song or other, but he had no breath to whistle.

Mason County Memorial Hospital dated from soon after the Second World War. It had become a little too small for the people it served. The emergency-room quarters had been expanded and expanded again and now occupied several inconveniently broken-up small rooms. No one seemed to notice when Martin came in. The admissions cubbyhole was vacant, but a cheap, squeaky radio was playing. Fiddles shrieking and steel guitars wailing, some country musicians rode like the hammers of hell into "Will the Circle Be Unbroken."

Martin sang with them absently, learning that he could at least still sing.

Well, his voice was no great loss to the live world, anyway.

Now that he was here, he realized what a tricky and annoying task finding his guitar would be. If it was here at all, it might be behind those doors, down any of those halls. He had no desire whatever to go near the morgue. God knew who or what was in there.

Question: How do you find a dead man's things without going near the morgue?

Next question: Once you find it, how do you get it out without causing a full-scale riot? As for that, he decided, by the time people calmed down he would probably be somewhere else, but the first question still baffled him.

Two nurses came into the shabby waiting room, apparently on their way to their lunch break. He stood aside to see what they would do or say. In their white uniforms they looked efficient and sturdy, afraid neither of pain nor death, nor of ghosts. He wondered once more about Jeannie down in Raleigh.

The first one said, "How was your morning?"

"Rotten," Martin said experimentally.

"Not too rough," the second nurse said. She was older than the other, though neither of them was young. "We had one brought in from a wreck. He hit the retaining wall out by Frazier's curve."

"Oh, God," Martin said.

"That's a shame. They ought to grade that thing away. It's a real deathtrap."

"It was all old man Raeford Frazier's stubbornness. He wouldn't let them build the road close to his house, so they had to make that big jog around it."

"It's a queer thing. Do you remember a couple of years back, when they brought that poor young girl in from out there?"

43

"Yes, I was here then. We couldn't save her; she was too far gone. And I never got the straight of it, either, why anyone would do a thing like that. I never saw such a reaction."

Martin, too, was a long way from getting the straight of it, but the nurses pushed past him and were gone. Another nurse came in to take charge of the cubbyhole. She said out loud, "Is there anyone here?"

"Yes," Martin said.

"Well, I just wondered." She began doing some typing, stared into space, ripped the paper out of her machine, switched off the radio, threw some more paper in, and started over. "I am so nervous I'm about ready to jump out of my skin."

Martin said acidly, "You don't know what nervous is, lady." He stalked into the inner reaches, opening door after door and closing them again, finding linen, equipment, empty bathrooms, examining rooms, X-ray machines, but nothing that had ever belonged to him. He swore.

Two women came breathlessly down the hall, one a nurse and the other in slacks and bedroom slippers, carrying a weakly crying little child. The nurse asked, "What did he eat?"

"I'm not sure. It was under the sink. My God."

"How long ago?"

"I just this minute found him."

"Did you try syrup of ipecac?"

"What's that?"

The nurse opened a box that said "Pediatric Gastric Lavage."

Martin quit opening doors. Enough, he thought. These people are busy. I really might scare someone to death. He bitterly regretted the loss of his guitar—for some reason all his sense of bereavement had begun to center around it—but it might not even be here at all. He would just have to do without it, unless he ran across someone who would help him.

In his mind the voice of the Frazier girl insisted, "Why don't you stay here awhile? I liked being alone, but it might be fun to have company."

It might, he thought. Or again it might not. She might be company. He no longer doubted her sanity. She understood the whole situation better than he did, but there was certainly something odd about her, and some story that was still going around.

An exit sign directed him to a different door from the one by which he had come in. But what now? He had been just about everywhere except the jail.

And the library. That was an idea. People would not stare at him there, and no one could make anyone nervous. He could hole up in the stacks—Martin had never believed he would find holing up in the stacks a welcome suggestion, but now it was definitely an idea whose time had come.

A pay phone hung on the wall by the door. He leafed through the skinny directory and learned that the library was on Spottswood Street, which he had crossed on the way to the hospital. How big was this town? No more than eight thousand or so. Once you learned which streets led from the square, getting around in it was child's play.

The library was newer than the hospital by some years, having been built at a time when federal money was lavish. It boasted floor-to-ceiling plate-glass windows and brick planters, which held juniper smelling as strong as gin.

This was a quiet time on a hot, close afternoon. Most people had gone back to work from their lunch breaks, and the children had not yet come out of school. As Martin pushed the glass door open, the reading room seemed deserted. No one was looking at the magazines or new book displays; no one sat behind the desk.

He was in a reckless mood by this time. You don't fire on the Red Cross, but the library lacked the sacred immunity of the hospital. If people noticed anything out of the ordinary, they would just have to scream, pass out, or do what they liked. He turned to the card catalog, hauled out a drawer, and began looking for an old book that had always been a favorite of his. He hoped it was in here. Unfortunately it had gotten a little bit out of date; so much grist for its mill had continued to proliferate. Its clear-headed skepticism seemed right now as salutary as clean air. It was also funny.

Steps crossed the tiled floor and a polite voice asked, "Can I help you find anything?"

He took a step backward and turned to face an old lady—a tall, still handsome old lady with the wrinkled face of seventy years and blue eyes that might have been thirty. She had spoken to him and she was smiling. "Excuse me. I didn't mean to startle you."

Martin got a grip on himself. "I didn't mean to startle you either. I've spent the whole day startling people, and I'm about ready for a change."

"Well, it's quiet and uneventful in here."

"It may not be that way much longer."

"No. The schoolchildren will be coming in, but by that time my assistants will be back from lunch."

"Are you the librarian?"

"Yes, I am."

"Could I just stay here and read awhile?"

"Surely. Why not?" She looked closely at him through her glasses. "Are you in some kind of trouble?"

"Yes, but nothing they can put me in jail for."

"Yes, I can tell that."

"What time do the others come in—the other librarians?"

"About twenty more minutes, if they didn't have a third cup of coffee."

Martin did not want to press his luck. When it came down to the crunch, he did not really want to bring on any screaming and passing out, especially on the part of this phenomenal old lady. He said, "I'll suggest that you not be found talking to me when they get here, unless you don't mind being checked into the nut farm."

"And why not, pray?" She actually said "pray."

The crunch had come. He gave her a doubtful look, which she returned calmly. He put his hand on her arm, which felt fine-boned and delicate through the thin sleeve of her dress. The blue veins were full and warm. She was warm as a furnace. Almost intolerably warm. He dropped his hand.

Then he said, "Don't scream."

"I have no intention of screaming."

"You'll scream when I tell you that I'm a ghost. I'm a ghost and you're talking to me."

She did not wince, burst into tears, or crack up with laughter. She just said, "Oh, no; I won't scream, even then. I might have known how it was with you. I would have known, if I had thought. So many dead, and so few come back, but I always know which ones they are. You want to ask how I know. You could say I have ESP. Or the second sight. Or that I'm old. Or just that I'm not stupid. Take your pick." Martin declined. "Do I know you? Am I supposed to? Do you belong to Masonborough?"

"No. I've never been here before."

47

"What in the world happened? No, you don't have to tell me."

Southern ladies, old and young. Martin grinned. Eaten up with curiosity and curbed by their relentless training in manners. "Basically, I had a wreck" —he decided not to go into the half-hysterical denial of his own identity— "but then I realized that something was really wrong and that no one could see me. There were a few other details, but that was it, basically."

"So you think that no one can see you now but crazy old ladies?"

That wasn't exactly right. "I believe the whole concept of crazy is going to have to be redefined."

"Maybe it should just be scrapped altogether."

"Maybe," Martin agreed. "Anyway, there was this one young lady. I thought she was crazy, but now that I've had more time to think, I'm beginning to think different. She told me her name was Frazier, but I forgot her first name. It was something odd, more like a place than a person. She came running out of her old house, there where I wrecked my car, and said that she lived there— rather, that she had been haunting it for two years. And I didn't believe her then, but now I do."

"Was she little and thin and flyaway-looking?"

"Yes. She was."

"Was her name Ashgrove?"

"Yes. That's right. That's what she said."

"Oh, I knew Ashgrove. As well as anyone did, I suppose. She would tend to make a good story out of everything, but she's not a liar. She probably has been haunting that place for two years. Yes. Two years is about right. That was a sad story," she added absently. "Such a mistake on everyone's part, starting with the old man, and no one knows where Raeford Junior is now, or

48

Francie Lee either," Martin fought down the urge, which he felt disgraced him, to ask exactly what the sad story had been. "Well," the lady went on, "if you see Ashgrove, tell her to come in and see me. She used to be a great reader, though rather undisciplined, like many precocious people."

When did he ever expect to see Ashgrove again? "Could I just stay here awhile and unwind?"

"Certainly, if that's what you want. As long as you care to."

"Thanks. More than I can say."

He looked around and a display caught his eye. It consisted of popular novels and nonfiction on the occult, possession, and survival after death. He was sorry. He didn't want to make fun of this lady's library. But it struck him funny. He leaned against the card catalog, nearly undone with held-in laughter. The blue-eyed old lady raised one chaotic eyebrow and her cheeks creased in a saturnine grin. She said, "Nobody ever went broke underestimating the taste of the American public."

"You're damn right, ma'am."

"It's gospel. The gospel according to H. L. Mencken. I frequently find occasion to mention it. Are you familiar with H. L. Mencken, young man?"

"Martin."

She accepted the correction. "Alice. Alice Kinsolving."

"Yes, I remember hearing about old H. L. He was from Baltimore, and so am I."

"He was one of the best things that ever came out of Baaltimer," she said, mocking him a little.

"Except National beer," Martin said, beginning to laugh again, but catching himself.

Alice Kinsolving turned to go back to the desk. She was silently laughing too. Martin hoped that the next person who came in would not worry about her, but did not doubt that she would cope. He located his book, Martin Gardner's *In the Name of Science*, dropped down on the floor in the farthest corner of the stacks, and read the afternoon away. People came and went, happy to pass from the heat into the air-conditioned library, but no one noticed him, for he was sitting in a little-used part of the nonfiction.

How quiet it was. You might almost fall asleep. He would not have thought that he needed to sleep. He fought against the desire. He shut his eyes and snapped them open. The room, the bookstacks, the quiet readers were all there just as before. He leaned his head against the wall and went on reading about the Flat Earth Society of Zion, Illinois. Now that was funny.

Someone threw the main light switch off and on to signal ten minutes to closing time. The few remaining patrons left. The lights went off again, leaving the library patchily lit by the hazy orange sunlight of late afternoon. The younger librarians said good night. No one was left but Alice Kinsolving and Martin.

He did not want to spend the night in the library. The truth was, he did not want to be alone, and in all the world there seemed only one place where he might not be, if he could get there again.

He came out of the stacks. "I have to go. Can you tell me how to find Ashgrove Frazier's house?"

She did not mock him, but said, "Yes, I think so." She led him to a large map mounted on one wall, which showed Mason County to be a rough lozenge shape, like the draw-a-diamond test done by someone who was not extremely bright. "This is an old map. But the Frazier place was there when it was made, and so was the railroad, though you can see that the federal highway was not. Which way did you come in?"

"I don't know exactly. That's my problem. Part of my problem. It might have been right here."

"That's the old road out of town. You can see that it twists and turns. It wasn't well surveyed."

"I'll say it wasn't."

"Well, the shortest way, it seems to me, would be to go down the main-line railroad track till you hit this east-bound road here. I would not go near Frazier's Crossing."

"What's that?"

"I just wouldn't go near it. I would drive you, but my mother will be waiting for me to get home, and she's over ninety. I could never walk that far, but you can."

"Oh, yes."

"Good luck. You know where the library is now, so come back."

"Thanks again," Martin said.

"Don't mention it."

"Who would I mention it to?"

"Me."

A police car had pulled up outside the library. A policeman—not the one from that morning—had come up to the door. "Miss Alice, I saw your car still outside. Are you all right?"

"Certainly," she said calmly. "I'm leaving now. Yes, I know it's way after six. I was just looking something up on this old map. Things have certainly changed since it was drawn."

The policeman held the door open, and Martin walked out close behind her.

"It's awfully hot, but it seems like there's a chill on the air," the policeman said.

"Yes," Miss Alice said. "It's getting late." She cranked her old Plymouth expertly and drove off. The policeman drove off after her. Martin turned back the way that he had come, to look for the railroad tracks.

The tracks roughly bordered the west side of town, where he had not been before. Here were the small businesses and industries that kept Masonborough going, grubby, workaday, and unpretentious—the lumberyard, the wholesale grocery, the fuel plant, the Southern States farmers' co-op, the Southern Coastline passenger depot, with only two trains chalked up on the board, and doing well to have that many. The westbound street where Martin found himself led over the tracks on a viaduct. The tracks themselves ran through a deep cutting. It looked like a steep climb down, but turned out to be fairly easy. The sides were thick with blackberry bushes, long since stripped of their fruit. He tried digging in his heels, but coming down holding on to brambles seemed to work better. I can't possibly weigh what I did before, he thought. Nor did the brambles hurt him.

He headed south out of town on the railroad tracks. He still greatly missed his guitar. Its familiar wooden heft and wooden-metallic voice would have been a great joy to him.

People made guitars. Banjos too. Even those three-string dulcimers. It might take forever, but he'd probably have at least that long.

The sun was nearly down, but the light had not left the sky, which was as colorless as it had been early that morning. The double right-of-way stretched wide to the south. Heat still blasted up from the heavy rails—he could sense it, though it did not warm him—and an odor of diesel oil and creosote. The breeze rose as the earth darkened and cooled. It might rain, or again it might not. Martin's hair did not blow and his shirt hung slack on his shoulders.

He passed a sign reading "Yard Limit." The last shabby outskirts of town gave way to the woods, a tall, straight plantation of pine, resinously fragrant and bringing darkness closer. The rails glimmered in front of him. There was no moon. Here and there was a block signal or a switch box, but mostly there were just the rails and the woods; no people.

Was that the moon? It wasn't the right time or place for the moon. It was a locomotive headlight.

Oh, hell.

The train came trundling and grinding on, not very fast, a slow, heavy freight pulled by one of those squared-off diesels. He could read the lighted number on the cab, but he could not see the engineer's face. The horn complained mournfully, blowing for the yard limit. Martin kept walking between the rails and the engine pushed him down and went right over him.

It took quite a long time to pass, and was quite boring. He had never seen the underparts of so many boxcars, nor did he ever expect to again. He found, lying under there, that he had oddly acute night vision.

The caboose lumbered off, and Martin got to his feet. He was not hurt, not even dirty.

I am really getting weird. I need someone to talk to.

He had thought that the girl called Ashgrove Frazier was a case for the locked ward and the straitjacket. He still thought that she was too nervous and talked too much and said too little to the point. But all day long, off and on, his thoughts had wheeled back to her when he wanted stillness and silence and understanding. If she could not give them, no one could, not even the remarkable lady in the library. Ashgrove had been as kind to him as she knew how to be, and told him as much truth as he was ready to take. At this stage, he would accept whatever she might give—truth or kindness.

# 3

ASHGROVE MOVED ABOUT HER BACK GARDEN, carrying a large galvanized can from which she watered her flowers. It was almost completely dark now. The colors of the day had vanished. Only the white petunias still showed pale, and you could smell them better than you could see them.

As the day had closed in, her anxiety had lightened. All was quiet now, except for the skittering locusts and her own slight voice. She sang, "Aquarius . . . Aquarius" as she hefted the watering can. It seemed appropriate. She had a good many plants to attend to: the bright-colored annuals, potted bulbs, tender perennials, an avocado tree, which had thrived outside and was nearly as tall as she was.

She did not hear Martin coming up, for his steps made

no sound. She was heading back to the pump with the empty can when she nearly ran into him. He said nothing. She could not read the expression on his face, but the way he stood told her that not very much still kept him going.

She thought that she might say "Ha," or "Goody, goody," or "I like your nerve." She said, "You're back."

"Yes. For what it's worth."

"It's worth whatever you want to make it."

"That and thirty-five cents will get you a cup of coffee. I'm tired."

"You didn't believe me. O ye of little faith."

"This is no time to be of big faith. People can't see you, you know?"

"I know."

"I'd never have believed it, but they can't. It's as if you didn't exist. They just look scared to death or like they might jump out of their skins. The only halfway sensible person I talked to was an old lady who works in the library."

"Oh."

"Then I decided that you were the only other halfway sensible person."

"According to my figuring, that makes a total of one."

"I'm sorry I was hard on you. I can sort of understand now why you stay here alone. Even a little town like that is terrifying. Too much going on and you don't have any place in it. I don't know which is worse, when they see you or when they don't. Even though the librarian lady was pretty sharp."

"Oh! I know exactly what you mean! Let me tell you about the time I ran away to the District. I mean, after I was dead. You think Masonborough is bad. The District is worse. The living are scary, the dead are scary, and those that don't know which they belong to are worst of all, let me tell you. Well, enough about that. I'm going to put you to bed. You need to sleep."

"I do not need to sleep."

"You just think you don't. You've done a lot today. You're worn out. 'For the sword outwears the sheath, and the soul wears out the breast.' Or is it the other way around? When I first came back here I was so happy I didn't sleep for a week, then I did nothing else for another week."

"I don't want to sleep for a week. You've got to wake me up."

"You'll wake up when you're ready. Come go with me. I'm going to find something to put over you."

She walked him into the kitchen, where from a cupboard she bundled out two voluminous quilts. They had to cross a breezeway to reach the main part of the house, where the stairs went up to the second story. The house was as large and shadowy on the inside as it had looked from the outside, and full of doors, all closed. The windows in those rooms let in no twilight now; only the rectangular panes that bordered the front door passed a glimmer into the hall. The upstairs rooms were all shut too. Ashgrove opened one. It was empty but for a dilapidated white iron bedstead that was literally held together with baling wire. She spread one quilt down on the dusty ticking. Martin fell in without a word, and she threw the other quilt over him.

He had meant to get up after twelve hours, but it took him more like thirty-six. He never heard Ashgrove leave the room. The quilts smelled of clean cotton that had been sunned on the grass. He slept as if he were trying to catch up on all the sleep that he had ever missed, and he never remembered his dreams.

Ashgrove left him alone. She knew far more about kittens than she did about babies, but she kept being reminded of an infant that sleeps away its first hours out of the womb, unreachable and needing no one. She tried to go about her business as usual.

As long as she had haunted her house, she had had much to keep her busy. It was still good weather for working outdoors. She always chopped her own wood and split her own kindling, never worrying about getting tired or hurt. What did worry her, to the point of near phobia, was the thought of fire. If she should lose her house she would have nothing. She kept her range and chimney scrupulously clean and had a tub of water always standing by the pump on the breezeway. In fact, the breezeway itself was a safety device; old country houses like this had often had the kitchen set off at the back to lessen the danger from fire. She boiled her candle grease outside in an old washpot. Kerosine lamps would have given more light and been less trouble, especially for someone who read as much as Ashgrove, but she was too afraid of kerosine to have it on the place, so she was hard put to keep herself in candles.

She needed warmth, and she needed light, and her live creatures needed care. In summer the plants took her attention, for during those hot days they would wilt unless they had a good drink every evening, but in winter the cats, outdoor creatures now, became extravagantly affectionate cold-weather friends.

The kittens had grown perceptibly in just a short time. Their eyes were beginning to open. They were the most beautiful, perfectly detailed little things she had ever seen, blotched with gray and black tabby markings like their mother. Their little paws dug into her sides and their little tails quivered as they nursed.

Ashgrove sang to herself, "The winter may go and the spring may die. . . . The summer may fade and the year may fly."

September was drawing in the light. Apples, rich and heady, would be rotting in the orchard, grapes in the wild woods. There would be drought, decay, and frost before green-sick spring brightened and ripened into summer again. Day to day—she would be all alone, and she would enjoy it all.

No, she would not be all alone.

Oh, ratsbane; I don't even dare play the piano now.

Maybe it wouldn't make any difference.

He's bound to get up soon.

I wish I hadn't remembered that he was up there.

How could I have forgotten?

She gave the plants their nightly watering, which involved so many trips to the pump that it took about half an hour. She fed the cats. That took very little time. Then she went up to the front room, where she kept most of her books. There seemed to be little that she wanted to reread. She chose a smallish box and carried it back to the kitchen, where she lit a candle and sat down at the table.

I shouldn't be doing this—it can't accomplish anything—but it makes me feel better somehow, more able to concentrate.

Ashgrove's treasure was a Rider pack of Tarot cards, which she adored with an uncritical fervor. Their sentimental illustrations took her into half-guessed, half-invented realms of beauty and terror unlike anything she found anywhere else.

She spread the whole pack out in front of her: kings and queens, knights and pages, greater and lesser trumps, overturned cups and broken towers, men and women climbing out of their coffins to hail the Angel of Judgment.

She chose one of the cards and laid it down. Then she shuffled the other cards, cut with her left hand, and dealt, murmuring:

"This covers you . . . .This crosses you . . . .This crowns you . . . .This is beneath you . . . .This is behind you . . . .This is before you.

"But this can't possibly be right," she said.

She chose another card, laid it down, and dealt again. "Mm," she sighed. "That's strange. Well, though much is taken, much abides."

She dealt several hands of solitaire then. None of them came out, there being no exact rules for playing Tarot solitare, but that didn't stop her from trying. Then she moved out onto the back steps, where she sat still for the rest of the night, watching the stars. In that smothering sky, the major constellations were all that could be seen: the cold polar stars and the hot Scorpion. She could tell by the sky and the stillness of the trees that it was still relentlessly hot.


Martin woke up, knowing it was daylight, but not sure what day it was. The bright quilts around him shimmered against his eyes. It was broad daylight outside, but at this hour—whatever the hour might be—only a slanting ray of hazy sunlight filtered in. The window was open. Vines and creepers crowded and bunched over the sill.

Then he remembered where he was. It didn't matter, then, what day. It was all true. The girl had brought him in here and promised that he would wake up, and he had. He got up slowly, feeling drained and cleansed, as though he had slept off a fever.

That girl is most likely downstairs. If she's still here at all.

Across the breezeway was the kitchen. He remembered

that too. Through the kitchen door he heard the sounds of sweeping and a cheerful but undistinguished voice singing:

> *"My gal got killed on the railroad track*
> *Two-miles-and-a-half out of town;*
> *Her head got caught on the drivin' wheel*
> *And her body ain't never been found.*
> *In the pines, in the pines*
> *Where the sun never shines*
> *And you shiver when the cold wind blows.*

"And the evening and the morning were the third day," she greeted him gaily. "Did you know it's morning?"

A rump-sprung wicker rocker flanked the stove. He dropped into it and said, "What's today?" He was wishing for a newspaper, the Washington *Post*, for preference. Putting its impressive gallery of comic strips between himself and the world might make him feel more civilized; who knew?

"It must be Thursday," the girl said slowly, "because day before yesterday was Tuesday, although normally I don't know one day from another. You want some tea?"

"Don't you have any coffee?"

"Afraid not. I could ask Jake for some, though, next time I see him. Couldn't I interest you in tea? I have right many flavors to choose from. Rose hip, spearmint, peppermint, sassafras, tulip tree, or sweet gum."

He wondered briefly who Jake was, but decided not to ask. "I just want something hot and strong."

"Fine." She scratched up the fire and banged down the kettle. Martin put his head in his hands. "Are you feeling bad?"

"I'm cold."

"I'll have some tea for you in a minute."

"I don't feel like I'll ever get warm."

She turned away from the stove. "No, I know; I don't ever really get warm either, and it's worse for you than it was for me. But you won't get much colder than this. You can get through the winters quite well without a jacket. Also, just think how ghastly hot it would be in here, if you could feel the heat! I don't know how we ever stood this stove. Why, in the worst part of the summer it hits the nineties in here constantly, I know it does. The cats' milk clabbers fifteen minutes after I put it down."

"Come here and warm me."

"I can't, Martin. I mean, I can come there, but I can't warm you."

"Come here anyway."

The girl looked at him with an odd expression on her face, which was small and nondescript like her figure. She stood in the kitchen of her house, where she seemed to belong. Her gaiety and self-possession attracted and annoyed him at the same time. Where did he belong? What was left to him? It wasn't any newspaper that he wanted. He thought he might feel better if he could touch her and hold her, insubstantial as she was, and little.

At first he thought she just plain didn't know how to kiss. Then he realized there was something more to it than that, something worse. This was not how a kiss should be. Their lips were dry and cold and unquickened by closeness. She was cold. They were both cold. They would never be able to get warm. She was wearing nothing under her sweater. She almost *was* nothing under her sweater, which looked heavy but wasn't. Horror advanced over Martin then and nearly blacked him out, and the girl knew it and he knew that she knew it. He thought that she felt the horror too. But neither of them dared let go of the other. She braced her arms around him. There was closeness after all. She was there with him. She was on his side.

The rocking chair easily held them both, although it was too broken down to rock well. She weighed almost nothing, but she could never have weighed much. He did not try to kiss her again, then or ever, but he still held her. He felt no warmer, but he did feel much less alone. He was comforted, and he was not. Whether the sadness he felt was his own or hers, he did not know.

He said, "What's wrong?"

"I don't know, it's all mixed up."

They spoke, not looking at one another, across each other's shoulders with their cheeks close together.

"Why are you so sad?"

"Same reason you are."

"It's hard to say exactly."

"Yes."

He shut his eyes.

She said, "Tell me what's really bothering you, and maybe I can help."

He felt the question was uncalled for. What was really bothering him? How could she even ask? Enough was enough. He dropped his arms from around her. Immediately she moved over to one of the straight chairs, and straddled it backward.

He said, "Everything I touch turns to shit."

She replied, "Try to think of it as compost."

He ignored that. "I'm just so damn cold." That was all the answer he could give her. He was cold all over where he used to feel warm; even his loins were cold and slack. Yet at the same time he was nervous and strung up. He had already almost forgotten what walking around in a body really felt like. He was a sensibility now, constantly noticing, half against his will, the sights and sounds and smells around him, and the restrained though powerful sympathy that was centered in the girl Ashgrove.

"You'll get so you don't mind it," she was explaining. "You might even learn to like it. Why, when I came back here I was happier than I ever imagined I could be. Of course I was halfway prepared for this, and you weren't. So I know it's a lot worse on you. Still, I'm cold. I'm always cold. I wonder about that sometimes. Did you know the ancient Celts believed that hell was a place of eternal cold? The Vikings too. Do you suppose we're in the Celtic hell? It couldn't be, though; it's too much like home. I just love ancient Celts and Vikings. Are you an ancient Celt? You have a Celtic name, don't you? The Fraziers were Scots originally, back in seventeen-something."

"I'm some Welsh, some Irish, some other stuff, and a little bit of Indian," Martin said, choosing the easiest question.

"Indian?"

"That's on my mother's side. She was from West Virginia."

"What part of West Virginia?"

"War."

"Oh, I know where that is; it's not too far from Grundy."

He began to realize that she was quite young, much younger than he had at first thought. Her confidence was that of a child, forthright and talkative, but keeping its own secrets. Experience—summers of tanning, winters of cynical grins—had whipped no scars into her colorless little face. But her mouth had a humorous set, and the lines of her forehead, cheeks, and chin, though immature, showed plain old-fashioned quality. Her eyes were the grey-green color of grass at summer's end, and they were watching him now with irony-tempered interest.

He said, "Now you tell me. You talk a lot, but it's all peripheral. How old are you anyway? What's your story? What really happened to you?"

She twined her arms and legs closer around the chair. "I don't like to talk about it. Maybe I'll tell you sometime, but not now."

"You're just a little kid. You're not more than sixteen."

"Well, I'm nineteen now."

"And you were how old when you died?"

"Well, seventeen."

"And you died of what? What kills seventeen-year-old girls?"

"In my case, something you wouldn't ever guess, I bet."

"People in town—in Masonborough—are still talking about you. Did you know that?"

"Well, I would certainly think they'd have better things to do with themselves by now. *I* don't ever talk about *them*."

"The nurses at the hospital even said they couldn't understand why anyone would do what you did."

"You better watch that, Martin. Being invisible to most people, you can get to be a real scandalmonger."

He stared at her, fighting down a sharp reply. He was stung, precisely because he had already sensed the danger of listening, looking, waiting unseen, drawing vicarious excitement from the crowded lives of other people.

The boiling water nearly shoved the lid off the kettle. She cried, "Ohhh!" and began to attend to making tea.

He said, "I didn't need that," and at the same time she said, "I'm sorry."

"Do you want to come sit up at the table?" she added. "It'll be done steeping in a minute."

He pulled out a chair and sat down across from her. "All right. We're both sorry. Tell me something else then. You don't weigh much of anything. Neither do I. How can you do anything? I see you holding that kettle. It's heavy. And I—" He decided not to tell her anything about the freight train. "Anyway, before I came back here, I had a rather far-out experience, but it didn't have any effect on me at all."

"What was the far-out experience?"

"Maybe I'll tell you sometime."

"Oh."

"It was really dumb. You wouldn't have thought much of it. Neither do I. So. What are the ground rules?"

"Well, did you ever use to get tired when you still had a lot to do, and wish that you could be pure energy? That's what you are now."

"Pure energy would blow everything up, like in Hiroshima."

"I'm not explaining this very well. It isn't atomic energy. It's some other kind. Maybe *nervous* energy. People were always telling me I had too much nervous energy and to stop fidgeting, but I haven't stopped yet. I hate the word psychic, but some people, who hadn't anything better to do, would call it psychic energy. Anyway, you're outside physical law."

"I'm here to tell you."

"You can act, but you can't be acted upon."

"How much of this did you read in a book?"

"Almost none. The books don't know. Did you ever read ghost stories?"

"Some. I don't like them."

"Neither do I, any more. All about things in the upper berth, and rats in the walls. Forget it. I don't do any harm. I'm just one of the ones who didn't quit."

65

"How do you mean, didn't quit?"

"How old were you?"

"Twenty-five."

"That's old."

"It's not old enough to die."

"That's what I'm trying to get back to. When you died, you didn't quit. And then there are the others—people with something on their minds. Fanatics. Lovers, madmen, and the untimely dead. Those are the ones who become ghosts."

"Well, but the untimely dead alone are in the millions." In spite of himself Martin was becoming caught up in the argument. "God knows. What about all the wars and disasters? Why isn't the world fuller of ghosts than it is of people?"

"Maybe it is and nobody knows it. There are certain places—like the old battlefields near here—where you'd never, ever get me to go." He had to agree there were places where you'd never get him to go either. "Except for one thing; I think many of them just drift away, sleep away into nothing. They're lonely and frightened and they finally give up."

"I could've done that—couldn't I?—just now."

"I figured you wouldn't."

"How'd you figure that?"

"Just did. You're too ornery."

"Thanks."

"Anytime. Then too, you know, so many people are religious. *I'm* not," she qualified, "but a lot of people are. They believe in some kind of heaven, so they must end up there. That's bound to be where my grandfather is. He was one of your rock-ribbed Presbyterian elders. Where else would he be? I imagine that's where all the women ghosts are too. You know how women are. They'll believe *anything*," Ashgrove declared. "I met a lot of men ghosts in the District, but almost no other women, except foul-mouthed old lady winos."

"I suppose you realize what you've just said: there's some overriding intelligence that hands out survival to people according to their beliefs. I don't believe it, but that's what you implied."

"I don't believe in anything—God, heaven, the church, or you name it. And don't ask me about it, because that's something else I don't want to discuss. It really distresses me, and I'll start crying. And I don't want to start crying. It's like priming a dry pump. You know: you don't have any real tears. Don't ever get in a situation where you have to cry. It's awful. It's like the dry heaves. Have you ever had the dry heaves? . . . Oh, ratsbane. Speaking of the dry heaves, this tea is going to be as strong as toothpaste."

She poured a cup for each of them. It was peppermint and did smell rather like toothpaste, but pleasant.

Martin did not care to press the subjects of God, tears, or the dry heaves. He said, "What's this? Cards?"

"Oh. Something I should've put away." She was on the defensive again, incomprehensibly.

He spilled the pack of cards out before him. They were a curious assembly of unfamiliar pictures, some with Roman numerals, some with names. The Fool, The Hanged Man, The Tower, The Lovers. A knight lay upon his tomb with swords around him. Another man lay on a dark shore, his body thrust through with more swords. Yet another, cloaked in black, turned his face away from some overturned cups. And a woman sat up weeping in bed with swords hanging above her.

"What *are* these? Don't tell me. They're fortune-telling cards."

"It's a Tarot deck. Forerunners to your regular cards.

67

See, they have four suits: cups, wands, swords, and pentacles. These are the greater trumps; they're extra. I love them."

"Where'd you get them?"

"Ordered off after them . . . Of course I know you're supposed to say you ordered them, but it sounds more portentous to say you ordered off after them."

"What do you do with them?"

"Just look at them. They fascinate me."

"I don't like them."

"Why not?"

"They're sad. What right do cards have to be so sad?"

"Life is sad. So is death."

"What do cards have to do with life or death? First you tell me you don't believe in anything, then I find you messing with this sort of junk. Do you believe there's some Big Cardsharp in the sky, or something?"

"No. It isn't like that at all. And they're not junk. They're like the illustrations to a book that's never been written. You can make up your own story." She collected the cards and put them away in a drawer.

Martin closed one hand around his teacup, which was still steaming hot, probably scalding. "I absolutely don't have you figured."

"What do you do when you have someone figured? Ring a little bell and out pops a tape?"

"Yes. It says, 'You are five foot nothing and headed for bad trouble.'"

"Oh, I almost forgot. I have a surprise for you. If you'll stop being ugly I'll give it to you."

"I don't believe I can take any more surprises, and I intend to go right on being ugly."

"Well, it's a nice surprise this time. You'll like it." She brought his guitar out of the far corner.

"I'll be damned." He had never expected to see it again, and was amazed that this high-strung rattlebox of an adolescent had thought to save it for him. "How did you get hold of this?"

"I hate to admit it, but I went down and helped myself, out of the wreck. I figured you'd never find it again in all the uproar and that this was as safe a place as any. I was counting on your coming back, I guess."

"Well, I suppose it's a good thing I did."

"Yes. I suppose it is."

"Apart from being way out of tune, it seems okay."

"You had it better strapped in than you had yourself."

"If I had been done in by some kind of violent reaction, I would not talk," Martin said grimly, scowling over his fingerboard.

Her eyes widened and her mouth seemed to tighten. If she were to call him a scandalmonger again, he would tell her not to repeat herself so much. There was a short silence, broken by sounds of tuning. Then she said quietly, "Play something."

"Just a minute, I'm still tuning." He plucked his E strings a few times and decided that should do it. Then he played a Spanish tune of intershifting minors and majors, which he had painstakingly taught himself.

"That's pretty. Thank you."

"Thank you. I thought this was gone forever."

"You're good. Did you study music?"

"No. I don't read music well at all." He was not that good and he knew it; he had started too late.

"What did you do then? Where are you from originally?"

"I guess I'll claim Baltimore. I had some college, then I was in the army. The last place I worked was in Washington at a music store. A good big one. Beautiful place."

"Do you think you'll go back to Washington?" Ashgrove asked.

"No. I don't know. I think not. I haven't decided what I'll do."

"I feel honor bound to point out to you that you can go anywhere you want to. Nothing to stop you." She looked skeptically into her teacup.

He supposed that there was indeed nothing to stop him, except for a vague feeling of inertia. No, more precisely, it was a reluctance to be around people but not one of them. In a way, his predicament was enviable: he had no need for money, food, or shelter. Need. There was a lot of garbage talked about need, windy generalities. You didn't know what you needed till you had it—or lost it, as the case might be. Anyway, the whole world was open to him now, except that he would always be an onlooker, like the soldier in the square. How short was the step from onlooker to scandalmonger? That was an ugly word, and unfair. He did not want to meet any more ghosts, either; Ashgrove was enough for right now.

"On the other hand," she added, "I'm honor bound to say that you're welcome to stay here if you want to."

"I might want to."

He did not know which of them he surprised more by saying that. This girl was a mess. She was terrible. But she knew something that he did not, though he was not sure what it was, and perhaps she could explain it to him.

She replied, "Feel free."

"You mean, be your guest."

"Same thing."

He took his guitar out on the back steps. His whole past life was coming back to him in bits and snatches of music, songs that had been popular to the point of exhaustion, played over and over on the speakers in the music store, on the car radio, in enlisted men's clubs on army bases, songs he had almost forgotten he knew.

> *Turning on the world*
> *the way she smiled upon my soul*
> *as I lay dying*

Start all over from the beginning, with what? He had his guitar back; he had a refuge, of a sort, and a fellow being, of a sort.

She was not watching him. She went on sweeping the kitchen, making an endless foray against the dust. The locusts seethed in the overblown greenness.

"Ahhh," Martin said, a sound of weariness and distaste. The girl was busy haunting her house. She would not come near him. He picked up his guitar, not wanting to lose it again, and wandered into the house, back to the upstairs room. He set the guitar against the wall and collapsed onto the bed again. Sleep took him. He dreamed and then slept past his dreams. The sun rode as far up the sky as it could.

# 4

It was noon of the next day, or thereabouts.

"Martin," Ashgrove said.

"Martin, it's really time you got up. You're making me nervous.

"I didn't really sleep for a week. That wasn't true. I exaggerated.

"It's been another twenty-four hours at least. That bothers me.

"Martin, please come back."

Ashgrove clenched her hands on the foot of the iron bed in the bare, shabby room. Martin slept. His length was strung out slaunchways across the bed. Except that he drew no breath and threw no weight on the springs, he might have looked like anyone who was deep in exhausted sleep. He lay neatly on his stomach, a swatch of dark hair crossing his forehead, dark eyebrows still drawn as if in bafflement or pain. For all his height and ranginess he looked as though he had not yet got all his growth and needed someone to feed him. His face was as old as it would ever get. The traces of his beard over the sharp edges of cheek and jaw would never be any heavier; the sunburn he had picked up that summer would never get any darker. The sun would not change him, nor would anything else, Ashgrove thought. He was only a trick of the light, a corollary to some little-known law of the universe.

She put her hand on his shoulder. He did not stir. She felt his cheek. No change. She joggled the bed. He flung out one fist as if to shove a car through its gear changes, and muttered, "Goddamn." Then he turned his face away from her. She pulled back the quilt and climbed into bed behind him, throwing her arm over his side and closing her eyes against his shoulder. She shivered a little. He was extraordinarily cold and far away.

She could not remember if his eyes were brown, hazel, or blue, largely because she had not looked him straight in the face any more than she could help.

He rose on one elbow and reached to pull the quilt up.
"Martin Evans. Do sit up and pay attention to me."
"My name is Evans."
"That's what I said. I said Evans."
"You said Ivins."
"Around here people named Evans are called Ivins. Do you know what you remind me of? The Dying Gladiator. Did you ever see that statue of the Dying Gladiator? We had a picture of it in an old book downstairs."
"Oh, for crying out loud."

73

"I was worried about you."

"Great." It seemed to him past time for that.

"I was afraid you really wouldn't wake up. Did you decide it wasn't worth it? It *is* worth it."

"Who are *you* to be telling *me* what is worth what?"

He spoke sharply, but she did not grow angry or defensive. They lay side by side in the narrow bed, not touching, each staring searchingly into the other's eyes. Then she said, "How can I tell you who I am? I have to show you . . . I know you didn't ask for this. You didn't ask to be born either. Both times you got something you never expected. It's amazing, the things that you get, and don't expect at all . . . I'm right here. Shhhh. You don't have to say anything." They held each other as through a siege of fever and chills.

Again he had the disturbing awareness of too many jumbled messages: great gentleness coupled with great concern and masked by inconsequent chatter and murderous irony. He also felt that she knew what he was thinking.

But she only said, "Are you comfortable?"

"Well, you're lying flat on my right arm, but given things as they are, it doesn't bother me much."

"I'm sorry." She shifted a little, trying to make him easier.

"I always thought there ought to be some better way, but I'm not sure this is it."

"What on earth do you mean?"

He explained, "Well, when you lie down like this, you know, with someone, after a while your arm usually goes to sleep. Good way to catch gangrene."

"Oh. Did you lie down with a lot of people, like this?"

"Not a lot. Some." He wondered if refraining from asking her the same question meant a point for him or a point for her. Still, he refrained.

74

She had slid down so that they were no longer face to face. He put his left hand around her chin, and she stared back at him. Then she broke into a smile of unfamiliar tenderness that wiped the sardonic quirks from the corners of her mouth.

"They look at you," Martin said, "but you don't ever know what's behind their eyes, and they don't ever tell."

"Do you feel any better?"

"Some."

"Things will come easier to you. With time. You have to give it time."

"Time. I have time. I have more than I know what to do with."

"That should be the least of your worries. There's plenty to do. Want to come with me? I need some wood. I always need wood. There are still certain survival things I need to do, you understand. This isn't exactly a carefree existence."

"Where do you get wood?"

"Off my land. Let me show you my land. There's still a lot of it. This is a good time to go, while it's dry. It's old and beautiful. I never get tired of it, even at this halfway time of the year."

Summer was disintegrating, falling to rags, its blue and green colors bleaching in the drought. The sun dragged toward its equinox. Its dusty light lay slanting on dry, pale grasses and patient, exhausted-looking trees, which still kept an uneasy equilibrium of summer greenness. Here and there the maples and sassafras showed red splotches, or high up in the tulip trees a yellow leaf flared like a quarantine flag.

A great untidy sycamore stood in the bulge of the road, braced by the front retaining wall. Its flung-down leaves looked like wrinkled brown paper bags. Martin eyed it with dislike. He had never cared for sycamores. They reminded him of some unpleasant place he had been— some army post or other—crummy wooden buildings and shabby sycamores, which never seemed to keep their leaves for a decent interval and always brought fall on before you were ready for it.

The closest woodlot lay south of the house, the land there sloping down to a draw where the creek ran; Shuttleworth's Run, Ashgrove said it was called. On the edge of the woods, sassafras held up its mittens; sweet gum went up like a skein of stars. Ashgrove said that in April the dogwood and the judas were something to see. Martin wondered where he would be by the time next April came.

They had to go back and forth often, because even with their tireless, wiry strength they could not carry much volume of firewood at a time. The barely surviving wheelbarrow was more trouble than it was worth; they used dilapidated bushel baskets that had once held apples.

Before you even got well into the woods, its air breathed out: damp, strong, and heady like wine, and like wine born from spoilage and corruption, drawing its rich acid tang from the rotting leaves underfoot: leaves of oak and hickory, strong with tannic acid; carbolic pine needles; and the sweet leaves of tulip poplar. Laid down on this layer like bits of enamelwork or oval scraps of red leather were sour-gum leaves; looking up through the yellowish-green tangle overhead you might find that a whole limb of sour gum had gone red as stained glass. Down by the creek there stood more sycamores, battening on the water, and elms underlit by water-flash. The creek was low, making its way slowly among the slabs of granite, but it was not altogether gone. Even the drought could not drink up all the waters of this countryside.

Seen just out of the tail of your eye, small animals and birds twitched and fidgeted, sometimes glimpsed, sometimes not. Once they saw a deer. It came down to drink in the creek late one hot afternoon. They watched it, fascinated, but it did not seem to notice them. Its ribs were corded on its smooth tan sides; its legs were thinner than anything ought to be. It trotted off, head held high.

"There are a lot more deer than there used to be," Ashgrove whispered. "This whole county isn't being farmed the way it was."

"Isn't this part of the country being developed like everywhere else?"

"No! Who would want to live here? Except me, I mean. Mason County is too far from the cities. It's isolated."

"Washington and Richmond are getting closer together all the time. Hadn't you noticed?"

"No, and I don't plan to."

"I still keep trying to figure out exactly where we are. Where does this creek go? What's the name of that river? I know it begins with R."

She laughed. "There's a whole lot of rivers that begin with R. You have to narrow it down closer than that. Let's get this wood on back. This always reminds me of Thoreau. He said his wood warmed him twice; once when he cut it and again when he burned it."

"Good for Thoreau," Martin replied. He was still cold, though keeping busy took his mind off it.

"I hate to think what would happen if this were New England. I don't really like snow. I don't know what all this New England bit is. Did you ever notice how when someone goes back to nature and decides to take over some old farm, it's always in New England? At least all the books say so. How do they stand it?"

"They want to be close to New York. And after all,

even New England isn't the steppes of Central Asia."

"Well, if they had any sense they'd come down here."

"You don't mean that. When people move in, first they come one at a time, but then the developers take over."

"Oh, horrors. Perish forbid."

"Let me tell you something else. The developers might not come, but the revenuers will. They're going to see the smoke from your stove and come roaring in to bash in your still. I don't know why they haven't come before."

"Some people did come once. Not revenuers. They brought a truck. I think they were after my banisters and chandeliers, to sell to antique dealers. People will take anything that isn't nailed down and a good many things that are. Probably wanted my bathtub too. It has feet. Well, I came out of the kitchen with my iron kettle in one hand and a candle in the other. They left. They about broke an axle getting out of the drive. No one's ever come back again. You notice I still have my banisters and chandeliers . . . Am I driving you nuts? My grandfather always said I was vaccinated with a Gramophone needle."

"No, go on. Tell me some more. What else do you do, apart from hauling wood and chasing off vandals?"

"Oh, plenty! Stick around."

She tried to show him what she did, in those first days. It was not really a whole lot, but it seemed satisfactory. She lived mainly in two rooms. Haunted two rooms? Used two rooms. He had already seen the kitchen. By day, plenty of light and air blew in through its screen doors and wide windows. The oilcloth and linoleum were worn but as clean as Ashgrove could keep them. Potted-up carrot tops thrived at the windows and a sweet potato vine cascaded from a knotted sling. The astringent scent of dried herbs in bunches and jars undercut the heavy odors of woodsmoke and candle grease. By daylight, if not by candlelight, could be read the homemade mottoes on the wall:

WHAT I DO IS ME: FOR THAT I CAME

*Et plus que l'air marin la douceur Angevine*

THERE WERE THOSE THAT WOULD HAVE WEPT
TO STEP BAREFOOT INTO REALITY

and a long one about "passions of rain, or moods in falling snow."

"In the wintertime, I put a sweet potato in a slow oven," Ashgrove explained, "and it smells heavenly all afternoon, and I read books, and the cats and I try to keep warm."

The front room was less pleasant; in fact, it was downright murky. It was on the northeast corner and trebly cut off from sunlight by the bulk of the house, the deep porch running outside it, and the vines, shrubbery, and trees that shaded the porch. Ashgrove tried, rather unsuccessfully, to brighten it with a heavy battery of candles. Besides an empty fireplace, which she dared not often use, it contained the ramshackle piano and a rump-sprung basket chair that was twin to the one in the kitchen.

Books, stored in cartons, gave a vague impression that a serious student was just moving either in or out. They were a motley assortment, which showed a wide generation gap. The older ones had evidently belonged to hardworking people whose education was nonetheless as important to them as their religion. A Scofield reference Bible, its binding in shreds. The Westminster Confession and Book of Church Order. Cruden's Concordance. Flavius Josephus. Almanacs and bound series of Sunday-school lessons dating back fifty or sixty years. School texts of Caesar and Virgil. Shakespeare, nearly as tattered as the Bible. *Pilgrim's Progress* and *St. Elmo*. Sets of Walter Scott, Dickens, Mark Twain, Kipling, and O. Henry. Then there were innumerable bright, shabby paperbacks, which betrayed an incorrigibly romantic taste: poetry, science fiction, British and American murder mysteries, spy adventures, and novels, none of the heaviest. Ashgrove, like those before her, had educated herself, and with different results, but with even more fervor.

From the high picture rail still hung a couple of sepia reproductions. They both showed women; one knelt on a rock, blindfolded and embracing a large stringed instrument; the other stood by a window, with sycamore leaves by her feet. Their names, Ashgrove said, were Hope and Mariana.

She was much more at home in this room than Martin was. He would pick a book that he thought tolerable, and carry it outside. She would vanish into the dim greenish depths of the front room, from which she could be heard practicing her piano, or trying to. It was not very systematic practice. Something called "Valse Sentimentale" was about the only piece that she could do up to speed. Everything she played was fraught with either mistakes or clinkers from the straining strings.

"See, when my mother left, she put a lot of stuff in storage—all the good furniture and Grandma's china—and threw a lot of other stuff out, but she left in kind of a hurry, and the moving men didn't want to move the piano, and it wasn't worth much anyway. So I got to keep it. I enjoy it. And I do the garden, keep the peonies and dahlias from getting choked out, fertilize, put lime on the hydrangeas. And play with the cats. But there's always something different. Now that fall's coming on, when the apples and the grapes are ripe and rotting, the whole place smells like applejack and scuppernong wine."

"What a royal waste."

"Of course I always carry Jake a couple of bushels, but he can't eat them all." Martin again ignored the mention of Jake. "Once we tried to make our own cider—and dandelion wine in the spring—but it just didn't work. Sad to relate."

"You honestly always stay here and never leave?"

"Well, I left once. I told you I ran away to the District and didn't like it. That was when my mother was packing; it was too sad; I couldn't stand it." He was not able to tell from her tone exactly what she could not stand. "Then I came back after I was pretty sure she was gone. I was so happy I never left again, except for short hauls. Oh, yes, there are ways to leave. You can walk—you don't ever get tired, except mentally—but it's easier to catch a ride in someone's pickup, or ride the train." She gestured vaguely toward the west, where the railroad ran. "I had a drawing room to myself all the way to Washington and back. And once I tried hitching a ride in a horse trailer. There was a horse in only one side; the other side was vacant. I thought it would be fine, but that poor horse started carrying on—kicking and hollering. I was afraid he'd injure himself, so I got out again."

"Oh, my God."

"See what I mean? Incidents like that. Always something. So I just stay here. Of course, sometimes I do tear across and visit Jake."

"Who is this person Jake that you keep raving on and on about?"

"I thought I told you about Jake. Didn't I? He's my friend. I've known him forever." She gave him an edited précis of her friendship with Jake. "Anyway, he can see me. He's been just beautiful about it, too. He's about the only person who's ever been able to. That is, if anybody besides you and him ever saw me, they never admitted it."

Martin began to say, "Well, Miss Kinsolving the librarian saw *ME*," but thought better of it.

"Anyway, you ought to come with me sometime and meet him. I know you'd like him."

"I don't want to meet anyone. Not now. I'm not proud of it, but that's the way it is."

He went off to practice his guitar. He had never had quite enough time to practice before. The instrument spoke to him with the familiar voice of a friend, the only tangible bit of salvage from his past life. He realized he might somewhat resemble the blindfolded lady on the rock, but it was past time to care about appearances. If Ashgrove noticed any similarity, she had the good sense not to say so.

Each of the five common keys had its own character: he had known this a long time, but now it fascinated him. *D* was delicate and gentle, *E* was gutsy. The bass strings nearly breathed for him. The treble strings whispered. When he was changing chords, they no longer squeaked and slithered under his fingers, but they answered his touch as well as they ever had.

Ashgrove sang with him sometimes, but more often left him alone. Her voice was willing but not strong, though she forced it to the limit. She was always singing to herself as she swept the kitchen or stood over the candle kettle, dipping wicks and tin-can molds barehanded into the molten fat.

> *"Just a Picture from Life's Other Side,*
> *Someone who had fell by the way . . ."*

Or then again:

> *"No, the roses they won't hurt you . . .*
> *Sally, don'tcha go, don'tcha go downtown."*

Martin finally got used to it. He learned that she had a wide and morbid repertoire and almost always sang the worst songs when she felt the best. When feeling unusually sarcastic, she might quote the Bible, but when deeply moved she relied on Shakespeare or other heavyweight poets.

The old house held him lightly. It had its own grace, though its off-plumb corners seemed to predate the use of a carpenter's square; it was not oppressive, for all that most of its dozen or so rooms stayed shut up behind their cross-and-Bible doors, their emptiness silting up in dust and spiderwebs, the stubborn vines prying the window-sills loose from the weatherboarding. Ashgrove explained that she could not clean everywhere all the time.

Bare heels flashing, she ran to and fro on her rounds, clattering the screen door or the stove lid. She found great comfort in concoctions of tea, though Martin still wished for some strong black coffee. She kept painstakingly busy in the garden. The front had all gone to weeds and rampant hedges, but the back she tried to keep scythed and weeded. "Every time I come back here I find some new kind of weed I never heard of. I think God must be running some sort of agricultural experiment station back here."

"You told me you didn't believe in God."

"I don't, but I complain about him frequently."

The cats charged in and out, leaping around on top of things or going to sleep under things. He learned their names. The kittens were growing. Their milk-blue eyes were fully open, but their little legs were too weak to run about much. He picked one up in his hand. It said "Pt!" vociferously. The mother stalked out of the box, lean as a lynx, with tufted cheeks and great lanterns of eyes. She sniffed anxiously at the kitten, which said "Pt!" again. He set it down.

"How in the world can they do that? Be so little and sound so loud and feisty?"

"I don't know. Made that way."

"They're getting wild as jackrabbits."

"We ought to pay more attention to them."

So on top of everything else they spent time with the kittens, sitting next to the box still faintly musty from their birth, coaxing them to be handled and gentled, and watching them whet their little teeth that gave no pain.

They figured that if they could think of anything funny, they were entitled to enjoy it. One of them could almost always crack the other one up. They laughed quietly and effortlessly, with no gasping, sideaches, or hiccups, finally reaching a stage where one dry word, the lift of an eyebrow, or the twist of the corner of the other's mouth would set them off.

They talked when they felt like it and kept silent when they did not. Ashgrove tended to break out into several paragraphs of anecdote and then say almost nothing the rest of the day. She kept her distance and he kept his. They touched little. She worked around Martin as if he were not exactly there, but she watched him, and he watched her. She was not the terrible mess that he had thought. She was a highly adapted intelligence and something to be reckoned with. He had tried to shake her, but he was glad now that she did not shake easily.

He had to admit that she was pretty funny.

"I always was," she said. "Only not many people knew it."

"Like when a tree falls in the forest and nobody hears it."

"Or like when Emily Dickinson had hundreds of poems put away in bureau drawers. Were those really poems, or were they not? I always wonder. Do they count if nobody reads them?"

"Depends on your definition. It's the same way with music. Bach wrote the *Brandenburg Concertos* for some old nobleman who didn't give a damn about them, and they molded away for a hundred years, not being heard by anyone."

"He had written them anyway. So had Emily Dickinson written hers. No one could change that. So there they were. Just waiting."

"And then there was Scott Joplin." But Ashgrove had not even heard of Scott Joplin, which tended to prove something or other.

Suddenly he thought of another odd young woman he had once met in the music store. She had wandered in, rather chunkily built, wearing a thick skein of hair down to what passed for her waist. He had asked her if she was a teacher. That was standard, for teachers got a discount on their music. But she colored as though he had paid her an extravagant compliment, and said, "Oh, no. I just go around telling everyone what to do." Then she paid for her music, collected her little girls, and left.

Ashgrove Frazier was another one who would go around telling everyone what to do; she was part great earth mother and part bratty kid sister.

He sharpened the ax and split kindling. It was very little trouble. He would have welcomed the job even if he could have gotten tired. It was pleasant here: sweet-smelling, placid, and immortally quiet. The noise of a car or truck whipping by, gearing down for the curve and again for the crossroad, was startling. He learned to guess the hours of the day by the sound of the trains, when he cared to guess at all. The sleepy, querulous voices of birds and insects could alone have told him the time of year.

Ashgrove did not tell him what to do any more often than he could stand. He supposed that sharing a haunted house with its barefooted lady, Hansel-and-Gretel fashion, was better than several other choices, like getting a sharp stick in the eye, for instance, or being stuck in the Baltimore Tunnel Thruway, or eternally driving around the Washington beltway at rush hour with no radio. Even *nothing*. The physics and metaphysics of his plight eluded him. He accepted each day as it came and the days were not, after all, so hard.

He surprised himself by caring enough to advise Ashgrove that her piano needed tuning.

"How could I have it tuned? Can't you just see a piano tuner coming out here? Even in the old days, a piano tuner was like a wandering gypsy. You had to know someone who knew when he was coming. Word got around."

"Well, you might throw some mothballs in anyway."

"So I might. I'll have to go get some from Jake. He's bound to have some. Don't you want to come? You haven't been off the place the whole time, even when we went after wood."

"No, thanks."

"I really want you to meet Jake."

"*No.*"

She did not press it. Well after dark, when the ten-o'clock train had gone by, she said, "'Bye now. I'm off to see the wizard," and took to the fields.


"How are things?" Jake said.

"Fine. I keep expecting him to leave, but thus far he hasn't. He seems fairly contented, so I have company on the place now. It keeps me busy."

"Back up and run that through again, will you?"

"I forgot I haven't been over here in a while, not since he came—the other ghost that I told you about. You know. You remember that day. Who could forget it? He came back."

"Oh."

"So I need some mothballs for my piano and some coffee for Martin. That's his name: Martin. And a grumly guest I'm sure was he. He says he wishes he had some coffee."

"Why don't you stay awhile?"

"I better get on back," Ashgrove said.

It was strange to be coming home and see the faint glow of candlelight from the kitchen. She banged in with the two small bags of coffee and mothballs.

Martin, elbows on the table, was reading an old copy of *Walden* with eye-destroying print. He said, "Here you come stomping in."

"*What?* I never stomp."

"It's an old joke. About a man with a hangover. He's sitting around, hoping to die and hoping not to, and the cat walks by, and he says, 'Here you come stomping in.'"

She grubbed in the back of a cupboard for an old speckleware percolator. "Now I'll tell you one. Did you ever hear of the dog who thought he was a duck?"

"*What?* No."

"I forgot; it was the other way around; it was the duck who thought it was a dog. When it hatched out, the first thing it saw was this big collie dog, which it thought was its mother. So it followed the dog around the rest of its days. Never would learn to swim or anything."

"No stuff."

"Gospel." She raised her right hand.

They fired up the range for coffee, which percolated richly through the kitchen. Martin said, "Ahhhh." Then they took the pages and the greater trumps out of the Tarot pack and played gin rummy, I Doubt It, and Go Fish the rest of the night. The games were more challenging since the unfamiliar suits were confusing. Neither of them slept. Martin was breaking the habit that Ashgrove had broken long ago.

A day or so later, on a breathless afternoon of gauzy sunshine, they had decided to take coffee outside and nurse it on the back steps. Martin had gone to the woodpile for stovewood. Ashgrove was pumping water into the percolator when she heard a car door slam. She told herself that it was someone passing on the road, until she heard footsteps and voices, coming closer.

There seemed to be three voices: two women and a man. One of the women had a southern sound to her speech, but the others were obviously from out of state. They were coming through the main house and onto the breezeway. Ashgrove tensed. She carried the percolator into the kitchen and began doggedly measuring coffee. Brandenburg strolled up, waving his tail. She said, "Where is the Hound of the Baskervilles, now that we need him?" Then she began singing one of her grandfather's more obnoxious songs:

> *"I've traveled this wide world over*
> *Ten thousand miles and more*
> *But a J. B. Stetson chamber pot*
> *I never did see before."*

The man and the women advanced into the kitchen. They were ordinary, well-dressed, well-fed-looking people. The woman with the northern voice said, "Well. It's a lovely old place, but it certainly is old-fashioned. Just look at that stove."

The other woman—smallish, fortyish, and very blond—looked baffled. "I can't understand why this wasn't kept locked. Howard gave me the key when he asked me to take you all out here. And who are you?" she added, turning to Ashgrove.

"I am Ashgrove Frazier and this is my house, as you are doubtless very well aware."

"I never expected this," the woman said faintly. "Howard should never have sent me here."

"Mrs. Yeargin! Are you all right? It's terribly hot in here, isn't it? My God, the stove's lit. Is there someone holed up in here?"

"Holed up! The nerve!" Ashgrove said. She pried up the stove lid, reached in for a piece of wood that had nearly smoldered to nothing, said malevolently, "Ha," and banged down the lid, thudding the percolator down on top of it.

At this point Martin, carrying a basketload of wood, wrestled open the back door. Sounding disgusted, he said, "Oh, jeez."

"It's happened. It's happened. They've come," Ashgrove said.

"All right, talk sense. It's not the revenuers. Is it the antique collectors?"

"They're going to sell my house. I know my house is going to be sold right out from over me."

"Quiet down. Look at their faces. They're worse scared of you than you are of them. What have you been doing? Performing with candles again?"

"Only this stick of stovewood."

"Oh, my God. Well, put it down. Haven't you any couth?"

"I'll put mine down if you'll put yours down."

"Well, I suppose I can't stand and hold it forever."

"I don't advise it."

He dropped the wood into the woodbox. "What now?" Ashgrove said, returning her ember to the stove.

"Have coffee," Martin said.

"I don't think I believe what I'm seeing," said the man from out of state. "I know I don't believe what I'm seeing. Mrs. Yeargin? What is all this?"

"I just don't know, Mr. Twining. I'm not sure I believe what I'm seeing either. Someone has certainly been here. It looks like they're still here."

"Please?" said the other woman—most likely Mrs. Twining.

"I'm going to put these cups on the table," Ashgrove declared.

"Why tell me?" Martin said. "I'm going to put some of that kindling into the stove."

"It's weird to have people watching you."

"I know. They're not exactly watching you. I don't believe they can see us. Maybe the little blond lady can, but not those others."

"I wish they'd leave."

"They will."

"Do you think that coffee will ever perk?"

"It will perk in the time that it usually takes, given the stove is as hot as it usually is," Martin said evenly. He shoved a few lengths of wood into the firebox, dragged out a chair, and sat down. Ashgrove's fingers flickered nervously. She fetched the coffee cups from the drainboard.

The three intruders still stood in the door to the breezeway. The couple called Twining looked as though they might faint. Little Mrs. Yeargin still had color in her cheeks and was smiling slightly. It was an odd smile. Martin wondered who would have to slap her if she got hysterical.

"Mrs. Yeargin, are you coming? I'm getting my wife out of here," Mr. Twining said.

"Yes. I don't think we ought to stay. This isn't any place for us."

She led the other two back the way they had come. They rounded the main part of the house rather than go back through it again. Ashgrove and Martin heard a car being cranked uncertainly. The engine finally caught and gunned off toward the Masonborough road.

"Don't come back," Ashgrove yelled.

"Don't be so vindictive."

"I am vindictive. Vindic-a-tive. I'm a venomous, vicious, vindictive, violent person."

"And vaccinated with a Gramophone needle."

"A Victrola needle."

They both laughed.

"We ought to go on the stage," Ashgrove said.

"Nobody could see us."

"Fit audience, though few."

"That coffee's bound to be done by now."

"Done to a turn."

They got their coffee, but it had little savor. They stretched out in the rank grass of the back garden, staring up at the checkered patterns thrown by the bear-paw leaves of the tulip tree.

"I didn't like that, did you?" Ashgrove said.

"No, I didn't, but it didn't really surprise me."

"They'd better not come back."

"Maybe they won't."

"Suppose they do. What will we do then?"

"I will not do anything except what I may happen to feel like at the moment."

"Well, I suppose that's the most anyone can expect."

"I don't claim to predict what anyone can expect."

"I expect we scared them off," Ashgrove said comfortably.

# 5

In Masonborough, people assumed that after Labor Day their lives might return to normal. The bloom was off the summer. It was tarnished.

Everyone hoped for rain, but no rain came. Sprinklers hissed on what was left of gardens, and air conditioners hummed and rattled. Brilliant cerise and magenta heads of bloom hung heavily on the crape-myrtle bushes, drifting their overblown fragrance over the town and making everything seem even hotter.

Out in the country, the farmers cleaned up after summer, harvesting and storing corn. There was a sickly sweet smell of silage on the air. Cows collected in what shade they might find from the day-long heat under lone sycamores and gum trees that grew by streams. The back roads were lumbered with school buses and large, slow-moving farm vehicles that had to be marked with orange-red triangles.

Miss Alice Kinsolving quickly glanced through the library copy of the twice-weekly Masonborough *Aegis* before inserting it into its display rod. The issue for the Friday after Labor Day mentioned a one-car wreck on a back-country road, the fifth fatality in the county that year. Miss Alice frowned, then bit down on a grin. Surely, wherever he had got to, Martin Evans would do all right for himself.


A young woman named Ginny Reynolds was talking long distance to someone she knew in Washington. She said, "Redfern, I'm beginning to believe you just don't know me. You don't know me if you think I would do that."

"Why not? It's easy. I can telephone one of the clinics up here and make an appointment."

"Oh, no, Redfern."

"*Oh, no, Redfern.* Well, you just don't know me if you think I would consider anything else."

"I didn't ask you to consider anything else," Ginny said slowly.

"Well, you have this number, so call me when you make up your mind. Because I imagine time is getting short and you wouldn't want to—"

"Sure," Ginny said. She put down the phone. Then she vomited into the kitchen sink. After that she rinsed her mouth, brushed her teeth, combed her hair off her forehead, and drove to work. She was a social worker for the Mason County Department of Human Resources, and she was about ten or twelve weeks pregnant. But she planned to continue that way in spite of Redfern, violent nausea, and everything else.

A little blond woman named Emily Yeargin looked into the bedroom mirror and quickly looked away again. Then she drank a large tumbler of cheap wine so that she could relax and get to sleep.

For some time, Emily had felt that there must be more to life than what she had. Yet what could she lack? Except children, of course. And children were a heartache, judging by the way some of her friends' kids were turning out. So you couldn't complain, could you?

Her husband was good to her. He never seemed to grieve over their lack of children. She had a beautiful home, which was very little trouble, since she also had a clever and reliable housekeeper. She tried to keep busy, but there was not much variety in Masonborough. She played bridge, though she was not very good at it; being dealt an excellent hand only made her nervous. She also helped with church work and made the rounds of bank, filling station, shops, and beauty parlor. She had an enviable collection of African violets. She read some and did a lot of fancy needlework. Her crocheting was always in demand.

Still, she was fond of Masonborough. It was not that she wanted to get out or live anywhere more exciting. She had spent several years away when Howard was in college and she was working to help put him through—in a college town that was distinguished from Masonborough by having a bookstore, one more movie theatre, and several more beer joints. Outside of that time she had never lived anywhere else, and doubted that she ever would. Howard's real-estate business had done well. He was proud of it, practically having built it from scratch.

Masonborough was growing—slowly, but it was growing. Howard's success was one measure of that growth.

One particular September morning, Emily slept late. The angle of the spots of light thrusting through the blinds of her bedroom told her that the morning must be well on its way. To what? To evening. She rolled over and sat up in bed, fighting sleep out of her eyes. Oh, dear. She had overslept again. Howard would have long been gone to the Commercial Café for breakfast. Why did she do this? But it was so hard not to.

At forty-some-odd Emily was beginning to look older than her husband, though there was little age difference between them. She had the delicate fairness that bleaches out early. Her clear skin was drying into tiny crevices, and her pale hair was passing unobtrusively from blond to gray. Her beauty had been that of coloring, for her features were irregular, and her bones were not big enough to carry the ten or fifteen pounds that she had lately put on.

She dressed quickly in stretch pants and a bright-printed top, not looking in the big mirror until she was ready to brush her hair and put on her makeup. Then she opened the blinds. Oh, dear, again. She could hear Mary Grace letting herself into the kitchen. Mary Grace, dignified and neat in her starched uniform, tended to intimidate. Emily could never understand what this intelligent woman was doing as a domestic worker, but she felt humbly lucky to have her. She suspected that she might not have her long. Smart people like Mary Grace always found something else to do.

Sun sparkled and glinted, thrown from wall to wall of the kitchen, bouncing off its pecan-wood cabinets and avocado appliances. Why does everything remind me of food? Emily wondered. She said, "Morning, Mary Grace.

Is there any coffee? Could I just have some black, with a banana?"

"You need Vitamin C too, Mrs. Yeargin. You also need more protein than just an old banana."

"I don't have time. I need to get going."

"For getting going, you need something on your stomach. Won't take but a minute to do you an egg."

"Please, no, thanks. Just coffee and banana."

"Well, before I leave I'm going to fix a special meat loaf for supper tonight, and I want you all to eat it."

"Mr. Yeargin thought you put too much wheat germ in the one last week."

"I'll put one more egg in this time," Mary Grace said.

Emily ate her banana dreamily, and sipped her coffee. Then she slid off her stool. "Thanks, Mary Grace. I'll see you at noontime."

"Will Mr. Yeargin be home for dinner?" Mary Grace meant the noonday dinner hour of small towns and country districts.

Emily thought not. "I'll drop by the office, and let you know about dinnertime, and we'll have the meat loaf tonight. Mmm. Your meals are so good. I'm really putting on weight."

"*That* isn't what's putting it on you. I know about all those wine bottles you hid in the trash."

Emily caught up her purse and keys and left. It was already hot. They were running the air conditioning indoors, and the contrast was uncomfortable. She sneezed. Then she drove her station wagon downtown to Howard's office, housed on a side street in a turreted white elephant, which she privately thought more appealing than her own shiny neo-colonial.

In front of the office a wooden signboard held movable letters. Today the slogan read: "Land is something that is not made anymore." She suddenly wondered, What if a great hand reached down out of heaven, and a great voice boomed, *That's what you think! Ha! Let there be more land!* Then she shook her head, promising herself not to tell Howard this; he might not take it too well.

Sometimes, if they were very busy in the office, they might find something for her to do. Emily loved the office. She had a shameless but innocent interest in other people and their houses. Indeed, it seemed that she lacked some faculty of judgment. Her liking for people and for houses was almost uncritical. There had once been an incident. One of Howard's listings was a middle-aged frame bungalow, perfectly ordinary except that it contained bees. The bees hived in the attic and generations' worth of honey had collected between the studs of the living-room wall. Exterminators could neither quell the bees nor remove the honey; one multiplied the other till the house swelled, dripped, and burgeoned like Jerusalem the Golden. Emily had thought this a delightfully unusual feature, but when she pointed it out, Howard lost the sale. Since that time, he had been wary of giving his wife much responsibility.

He was glad to see her today. He said, "Hi, honey," and gave her a kiss. Emily was short, but Howard was not much taller. His driving energy was such that he seemed larger than he really was. He smiled at her kindly. He had a beautiful smile, she thought. In some ways he looked younger than ever, since he had let his hair grow longer. The close-cropped, smooth-faced boy in old snapshots now seemed a stranger, almost like a convict or a mental patient.

"Honey, listen." (Howard had always called her honey; no embarrassing reference was meant.) "Usually I don't like to bother you with these things, but can you take someone out to look at a house today? You know the county, and we're all tied up."

"I'd love to. You know I would."

"Now listen. This will be perfectly simple. Nothing is wrong with this house. No bumblebees. No wet cellar. The wiring and plumbing are old-fashioned but sound. It's a real jewel. The old Frazier place." He showed her the page in the listings book.

"Yes. This is a nice one. Look at all those porches and windows. And the trees! Yes, I know where that is."

"Well, a Mr. Twining called up—he's an executive at that new chemical plant outside of town—and he and his wife are looking for something unusual, and this might be it. I'd like to get it moving, because not everybody would be interested. Francie Lee Frazier evidently just got the title clear."

"Fine, Howard. I'll be glad to. What time do they want to go?"

"Can you make it about two? Well, you meet them then, at the Holiday Inn."

"This must be a very historic county," Mr. Twining said.

"History, that's what we're interested in," said his wife.

"Well, to tell the honest truth . . ." Emily began. Then she stopped. It was usually better to ask questions than to make statements. "What kind of history?"

"Oh, every kind. All the wars—and famous people— and ordinary people too. We're great collectors of antiques. I love the things that people have really used— churns and flatirons and so on."

"Well, I suppose in Mason County you'll find most of us pretty ordinary, except we don't use churns and flatirons."

"It's really not a bad drive out from town, is it?" Mrs. Twining went on. "You could even drive in and spend the day in Washington if you wanted to. Or Richmond."

"If the traffic didn't kill you," Mr. Twining said.

"Well, here we are," Emily announced, warping her station wagon through the overgrown gap in the hedge and up the potholed drive.

"My. It's certainly old."

"Of course it needs paint."

"I could tell you someone in town who would be glad to come out here and paint it."

"This yard needs a heck of a lot of work."

"Do you think there's anyone in town who would come out and do the gardening?"

"Let's see the inside before we decide on all these other plans."

Emily brought out the bunch of iron keys that was dragging her pocketbook down. "The door isn't locked. Someone from the office must have been out here before. I wonder why they didn't put a lockbox on it."

"*Mmm.* What is that blooming? Honeysuckle and something else." Mrs. Twining did not recognize clematis, but she appreciated it when she smelled it.

"Now I don't know exactly what we'll find in here. Most of the furniture was stored, but there may be a few old pieces left."

"*Dusty.*"

"Even when you leave a place clean, dust does filter in," Emily said gently. "Now down here, as you see, there's the front hall, living room, dining room, and two extra rooms that could be bedrooms or anything you wanted."

They admired the green slate fireplaces and the built-in cupboards in the dining room. They did not admire Ashgrove's books or her piano. "What people leave behind. It's unbelievable. Didn't they want them?"

"Upstairs there will be four bedrooms, a big hall, and a bath."

"Only one?"

"I imagine we could put in others."

"Certainly. My husband says the plumbing is adequate."

"What about the kitchen?" Mrs. Twining asked suddenly.

"Let me check my keys. The kitchen would be at the back, across this breezeway." Here was another unlocked door; really strange. "That was how they used to build them; fire was such a threat out in the country, you know, though not any longer, now that they have the volunteers," she added hastily. "This breezeway is a lovely place for plants, if you have plants." Emily frowned at the galvanized tub full of clean water, which sat next to the old pitcher-pump. That had surely not been here for as long as the house had been empty.

Then she realized that the door from the breezeway to the kitchen was not only unlocked, but standing wide open.

The Yeargins argued all through their meat loaf, hardly tasting it.

Emily cried, "Howard, bees are one thing. Wet cellars are one thing. Termites are one thing. Ghosts are something else."

"Emily, I don't know what makes you carry on like this. You imagined it."

"I did not. I know I didn't. You can ask the Twinings."

"Are you kidding? I'm even embarrassed to go near them."

"I'm sorry about that. I really couldn't help it. It wasn't

100

my fault. And I behaved very well, considering. Mrs. Twining was the one I was worried about."

"You're proud of that?"

"Oh, Howard."

"Oh, hell. Well, I'll have to do something about it. I'll have to go out there, and see what's actually going on, if anything, and I can't go before late tomorrow afternoon."

"Let me come too."

"All right. I guess it won't do any harm. Any more harm. And now I don't want to hear any more about it."

The strangest, most enthralling experience of Emily's life, and her husband did not want to hear any more about it. She slept, fortified with wine, while Howard watched the late movie. The next day she considered writing to Ann Landers. But she could never write down all that had happened without getting into endless snarls of qualification. For instance, what really *had* happened?

She just thought it was time to talk to someone.

There was Mary Grace, quiet, dignified, and efficient.

"Mary Grace, do you believe in ghosts?"

"Well . . ."

"I really want to know. I'm not trying to make a joke."

"Well, my mama, she told me some strange things her mama had told her."

"Do you believe there are *still* ghosts—not just from our mamas' time?"

"Could be."

Emily fidgeted.

"What's on your mind, Mrs. Yeargin?"

"Well, yesterday . . ."

"You'd better tell me, hadn't you? I can tell you want to."

Emily tried. Mary Grace listened patiently.

"I don't know how I knew they were ghosts. I just

101

knew. Like in the movies when someone is playing a double role or they're using trick photography. Sort of like that. They didn't look quite right around the edges; they didn't catch the light right, and they didn't throw any shadow."

"I don't even believe Mr. and Mrs. Twining could see them at all. They claimed they couldn't. They were in right bad shape. But other than that it wasn't frightening. I mean, you would think of a haunted house as being all covered with bats and cobwebs . . ."

"Scary organ music," Mary Grace suggested.

"But the kitchen, the part they seemed to be using, was *clean*. It looked *lived* in, if you can imagine that."

"Maybe it was lived in. Maybe it's not haunts at all. Hippies or something. Squatters."

"Well, I saw them, and I knew they were ghosts and not hippies, though the girl was barefooted, and he was wearing those old blue work clothes. And then, when the girl told me her name was Ashgrove . . . I didn't tell that to Howard. He cut me off too fast, and acted ugly. But I'll have to tell him. Maybe he'll believe me then. Or maybe he'll think I'm making it up more than ever. I don't know. I didn't recognize her at first. I only used to see the child at church sometimes, wearing a little short dress over those little skinny bare legs, and glaring around like she'd rather be somewhere else."

"Ashgrove, hm," Mary Grace said thoughtfully. "Who was the other one? One of those other Fraziers?"

"No. I didn't recognize him at all. It was a boy, though—rather, a young man. He would have been nice-looking if he had been better dressed. It was right funny, Mary Grace. They were just going about their business when we walked in. Do ghosts drink coffee?"

"I've heard that they drink it hot, right out of the spout. But that's old haunt tales. I don't believe it."

102

"Anyway, she said to him, 'What now?' And he said, 'Have coffee,' just like Howard might. And we left."

"That was the best thing you could have done. You ought to leave them alone. Messing around isn't going to get you anywhere."

"Howard can't sell a haunted house."

"What's he going to do then? Burn it?"

"That's not the only reason why I'm upset. Not just the worry about the money. I—" Emily halted. She still could not find words for the attraction working on her from the house, haunted or not. "I felt that there was something I could do."

"What can you do? You have nothing to do with them, Mrs. Yeargin." Was that advice, or a plain statement of fact?

"They could have been my children, if I'd had any," Emily said. "Maybe not. Maybe I'm not quite that old yet. Do you have any children, Mary Grace?"

"Yes, ma'am. Two girls. They're doing good. The youngest one's in college."

"That's grand." Emily wondered why she had never asked that before. Mary Grace listened to her confidences, but she never offered any herself. Then Emily asked if they needed anything from the grocery store, and Mary Grace handed her a neat list. She wandered out to her car and went shopping.

Emily preferred to shop at an independent grocery called Mac's Little Giant. It had better meats and prettier fresh produce than the big chains, and Mr. Mac was one of the last of the old-time merchants, always ready to wait on you himself, and asking you if everything was all right. And it seemed that it usually was. Mr. Mac's place was clean and healthful, and Mr. Mac was . . . what? Safe and sane, maybe, like the Fourth of July. Emily beamed at the sight of his round red face.

"Hi, Mr. Mac. How are you?"

"Hi, Miss Emily. How are you?"

"Just fine. Except I keep having these funny experiences." His chuckle encouraged her. "Mr. Mac, do you believe in ghosts?"

Mr. Mac lost his cheerful expression. "No. I do not. And I would advise that you do not. There's nothing funny about it."

"No. No, I guess I never really thought there was," Emily said meekly. She finished paying for her grocery order and Mr. Mac carried it to the car for her. She thanked him, but he returned her smile absently.

Not till she was putting the groceries away did she remember that there was some story about someone in Mr. Mac's family—was it his cousin or great-uncle?— someone who had been killed violently and was said not to rest in his grave.

"Oh, mercy," she said.

Poor Mr. Mac. He was the last person I should have asked.

That was such a long time ago. I wish I could remember all the story.

I just wish I could feel that I wasn't the only one who knew or cared about this.

Well, maybe something else will happen when I go out there with Howard this afternoon. Something different. Something real. No, that's not right. I don't know.


"Was that an engine?" Ashgrove said suddenly. She had been lying in the grass, reading *The Lord of the Rings* for about the dozenth time, but she jumped to her feet and peered around toward the front of the house. "Martin! It's some more people. Again."

Martin moved fast. He snatched up his guitar and took

Ashgrove's elbow in his other hand. "All right. This time we're leaving. We're not staying here to be gawked at."

"I like your nerve."

"Come on. Act like you had some sense."

They spent the rest of the afternoon at the far edge of the orchard. Ashgrove fretted desperately, for she hated to miss whatever might be going on, but Martin was adamant.

"There isn't anybody here," Howard said.

"Somebody has been, " Emily said.

"Yes, I grant you that, somebody has been. I wonder how they got in. They don't seem to have done any damage."

"Damage! They've improved the place! Did you see those flowers in the back? That took a lot of time and patience; whoever put those in can't be all bad. Look how clean this old stove is. I sure wouldn't want to have that job. And would you look at this?"

She got to her knees to look at the cat family. The kittens were peeping out of their box. One of them dropped over the side. The mother made a sound, got out, and retrieved it by the scruff of the neck.

"Great God," Howard said. "This is too much."

"Poor little cats. You leave them alone. They're harmless."

"Oh, for Pete's sake. I'm going into the other part of the house and check the upstairs. You want to come?"

"No. I'll stay here. I'm not afraid to."

"Suit yourself."

Howard left the kitchen and went into the main house. He had no trouble, for all the doors were unlocked.

Left alone, Emily whispered, "Ashgrove?" There was no answer. "Ashgrove?" she said more strongly. Still nothing. Afternoon light flooded the windows and printed leaf shadows on the walls. She gazed in bemusement around the kitchen, examining the iron teakettle and the speckleware coffeepot, the cups and saucers on the drainboard, the plants and the mottoes. Then she began opening all the cupboards, finding nothing but cat food, dried milk, and a few more odd bits of crockery, glass, and tinware.

Howard returned. "There's nobody up there. Most of the rooms are full of dust. I'd almost swear nothing had been touched in years. There aren't any footprints in the dust. At least there aren't any piles of human garbage and no empty bottles of Rose of Tralee either."

"Howard."

"*What?*"

"I looked in the cupboards and there's nothing there except food for the cats."

"So?"

"The people here don't eat. Only the cats."

"They probably went out grocery shopping. That's probably where they are right now. Well, they're going to get a surprise. You sure haven't proved to me that there are any ghosts here, Emily. I'd never believe a thing like that till I saw it. Probably not even then."

"You probably *wouldn't* see it. That's what would scare you."

"I imagine they're people from the city looking for a free place to stay. Hippies and dropouts."

"That's what Mary Grace said. But she didn't see them, and I did."

"Have you been talking about this to Mary Grace? What on earth for?"

"She seemed kind of comforting, though I don't know why that should be; she's so solemn."

"Boy, look at this artwork, will you?"

"I have been looking at it. And listen, Howard. One more thing. Did you see any garbage cans?"

"What's that got to do with it?"

"You can tell a lot about people from their trash. The FBI goes through people's trash all the time." And then there's Mary Grace, she thought. "There ought to be some cans right around here. But I didn't see any. Did you?"

Howard shook his head, looking impatient to be gone.

"And there's no trash lying around the back door, either."

"Well, I'm going to lock this place up tight as a drum and put "No Trespassing" signs all over it. Then we'll call the sheriff if we have to."

He brought water in the kettle and soundly drenched what fire remained in the stove.

"Howard, you can't lock up those cats in here."

"Oh, all right. Come on, cat." He picked up the whole box of cat and kittens and moved it onto the breezeway. Emily followed with the boxes of food. While he made the rounds with the ring of keys, locking doors, and putting up signs that he brought from the car, she fed the cat and filled its water dish. As they drove back to town, Howard seemed pleased, feeling that he had attacked a problem and begun to solve it, but Emily was thoughtful and jumpy by turns.

When Ashgrove found her house locked against her, she calmly reached under the back steps and came up with another key—actually a pair of keys, wired together. One was an extra key to the kitchen; the other was a skeleton key that with a little forcing would turn the other old-fashioned locks. She said that they were her secret weapon of years' standing. Then she returned the ousted cat family to the kitchen.

"Whoever did this can't be all bad," she said. "They even left some water for poor old mama cat."

"It was a man I'd never seen before, and the same little blond lady from the other day," Martin said. "I saw that much of them."

"It's all really quite strange."

"Something is evidently happening in the outside world, but you don't know what it is and can't do anything about it."

"This is my house, and I'm going to haunt it. They can't sell it out from over my head."

"They don't know your head's even here. Or care. Look at it this way: They may not be able to sell it, even if they want to. But even if they do, you can still haunt all you want too, I suppose."

"That's just it. I don't have any choice, even if a family of *fifty* moves in."

"Yes, you do. You always have a choice. You can leave."

"Leave? How? When you're a ghost, you haunt a *place*. And this is my place."

"You know, theoretically, you could go anywhere. The whole world is open to you. I still think about California, San Francisco especially, but it's all beautiful."

"I didn't know you'd ever been in California."

"I didn't stay there long. I got a better job in the District, and sort of wanted to be on the East Coast anyway. Decided I'd go back to California when I'd saved some money . . . Of course, I don't need money now."

"San Francisco is cold."

"The sun is warm."

"It's foggy."

"I remember."

"The San Andreas Fault, I read, is going to break it off and slide it into the ocean."

"I read that too, but there'll still be a lot left out there."

"Martin, you can go anywhere you want to, any time you want to, but my place is here." She added brightly, "Why *don't* you leave?"

"I have done all the talking about that I'm going to do."

"Well, I'm going to leave these signs up, because I don't want any trespassing either. Imagine the nerve! People coming picking around on my land!"

Martin said sharply, "You have no title to this land. The only land you own is a place in some graveyard."

"I am *not there*." She added as if by reflex, "I am risen."

He let this sink in for a few seconds. Then, just as automatically, he glanced up as if to ward off a bolt of lightning. They both broke up laughing.

"It's not funny," he said finally.

"Then why are you laughing?"

"Same reason you are."

"Can't dance, and it's too wet to plow."

"Right."

"It's not too wet at all. I sometimes wonder if it will ever rain again."

The sun was sinking, a disk of tinfoil pink that gave no radiance to earth or sky.

Emily went on her rounds distractedly. Everyone she met she wanted to ask, "Do you believe in ghosts?" Some people—those she had known a long time and felt she might more easily confide in—she actually did ask. The reactions were varied.

"No, but I always wanted to see one."

"Emily, you're getting batty. Is it time for your lady troubles already?"

"Ha!"

109

"Why, yes, I do. Let me tell you about this thing that happened to someone in my family. . . ."

"Spooks? The only spooks I know about are those they're sending to school with our children."

"It's of Satan. It's definitely of Satan."

"Oh, I wish I could believe."

Miss Alice Kinsolving, adjusting her glasses like a lorgnette, said, "Why do you ask, pray?" This unnerved Emily, who said, "No reason," and left the library, taking with her a large book on the occult, which she found heavy but encouraging.

The Twinings took their business to another, larger realty company. They ended up buying a house in the next county, which was considerably closer to Washington. For twice what they would have paid for Ashgrove Frazier's house, they got a large, eagle-ridden colonial in a brand-new development with no ghosts and no trees. Mr. Twining commuted to his executive job at the new chemical plant outside of Masonborough. During all the smothered excitement that followed, rampant rumor and garbled publicity, they never mentioned to a soul what they had seen, or not seen. They merely said they were glad they had decided not to rough it in that old farmhouse.

Emily, however, could never be sure that they would not talk, and to ruinous effect. The rival realty company could gleefully give all its customers the impression that Howard Yeargin handled haunted houses, bursting at the seams with the most nerve-destroying phenomena. She began dealing in a little counteroffensive propaganda; she felt it was necessary, and she had no more sense than to want to talk about what was important to her. "Did you hear that there was an incident of haunting in one of

Howard's houses? You didn't? Well, let me explain to you what really happened. It wasn't as bad as you might think . . . Yes, it's true. I was there. Let me tell you about it so you'll know exactly what went on."

Telephones rang off the wall. "When can we go out there and see it?" Mary Grace took messages calmly, accurately, and without moving a muscle in her face.

Howard said, "Emily, we're trying to move houses, not run a damn tour. I don't know how these stories get started, and I hope I never find out."

Emily said, "Howard, the house is haunted. You'd better let people know the truth before they think up something worse."

"What could be worse than that?"

"A lot. Remember when old Mrs. Shuttleworth died and nobody knew it for a week and the firemen had to put on their oxygen masks and go in and get her out?"

"Oh, great God, Emily! Anyway, it is not haunted. I put lockboxes on it, and when I went back to check, nobody was there." At that time he had hammered in a FOR SALE OR RENT sign with the determination of Martin Luther nailing up theses. "The cats had been taken away—or run off—but nothing else was changed."

"You hope," Emily said.

What she herself hoped was different; she hoped that those two ghosts would somehow get back into their house—maybe they could walk through the wall?—into the kitchen where they seemed to dwell in such baffling domesticity. Howard needed to sell the house. They could use the money; you could always use money; she wasn't fool enough to think that you couldn't. But didn't the ghosts also need a place to stay? Perhaps the old kitchen could be given over to them and a modern one built in the main part of the house. No, that didn't make sense. But what did make sense? Precious little.

What were they waiting for, in there? Was there something they wanted?

Hot as it was, hardly a day passed that someone or other did not drive out to peer around the Frazier house. Howard was furious, for he was sure that no one wanted to buy it. Many of those who went to look were, in fact, curiosity seekers, hardy souls, or just bored. It was a boring time of year, anyway. The few who were really in the market to buy were put off, or said they were, by the age of the house and its remoteness.

The talk persisted, though no one had seen much to talk about.

It was the older people who were talking. Those of Ashgrove's contemporaries who were still living around Masonborough never said anything. The subject was too close to them, or too complex, though none of them had been very close to Ashgrove, the smallest, smartest, most uncoordinated, and most flatchested of her entire junior class. The most any of them would say was that the older generation was acting screwy as usual.

Martin Evans' parents buried their next-to-youngest son and tried not to talk to each other about him any more than they could help.

If the people who had made the ill-fated raid on Ashgrove's chandeliers and banisters were still around, they never came forward.

On the other side of the law, the young policeman named Roy said nothing either. His contact with a ghost had been the most terrifying and the least explainable. He had a wife and a baby and he wanted to keep his job. If he ever connected his experience with those of others, he never told anyone.

Howard Yeargin would dearly have liked to call in the

sheriff, but since no damage could be proved, he decided not to. He just wanted to get the place tenanted. Then any disturbance would be the tenants' problem.

Emily's family and Howard's practically stopped speaking to each other.

Alice Kinsolving thoughtfully nibbled the frames of her glasses. She was of a good mind to drive straight out to the Frazier place and take a look herself, but she hated to be classed among the thrill seekers. Deciding to seek counsel instead, she picked up the phone and called her minister. He and his wife were old friends of hers, though not that old; they were ten years or so younger than she. They had come twenty years ago from South Carolina, which was not quite the same as Virginia, but almost as good. Anyway, by this time, since Presbyterians didn't move their clergy around like chessmen, the Gilchrists surely counted as honorary Virginians.

"Charles? It's Alice Kinsolving."

Mr. Gilchrist said, "It's good to hear you."

"How's Helen?"

"She's fine. How's your mother?"

"About the same."

"I'm sorry."

"It's all right. Nothing you or anyone can do. Fortunately the doctor keeps her comfortable. Charles, what do you think of all this supernatural chatter? Haven't you heard all the talk that's going around? About the Frazier child? Surely you must have."

"Yes, but I didn't pay much attention to it."

"Don't tell me you thought it was of Satan."

"I didn't even dignify it as much as that."

"Well, you'd better dignify it. There's something to it."

"Miss Alice."

"Listen, Charles. You know Emily Yeargin is trotting

around saying that there are two of them out there. A young man as well as the Frazier girl."

"Yes, I had heard that," the minister admitted.

"Well, you know Emily. She's romantic," Miss Alice said witheringly. "I know exactly what sort of stuff she reads; I know exactly what sort of stuff everybody reads, and I always will know, until we get one of those new checkout systems. But that's by the way. Anyway, Emily describes Ashgrove Frazier as you and I remember her, which isn't that easy, for there was never that much of Ashgrove to describe, and she says that this boy is tall and dark-haired and good-looking. Of course, Emily would say that. She would have to say that. I wouldn't. He had a sharp-tempered, lantern-jawed look on him. But I saw him. Don't hang up. You think that you're going to phone my doctor and have me certified, but you're not, because I'm still smart enough to look after my mother as well as this library, and everybody knows it."

"Go on; I'm listening."

"Do you remember that wreck a week or so ago?—ten days?—when was it?—where someone from out of town was killed on that back road by Frazier's place? You can check your newspapers if you don't believe me. Or I'll check them for you. That very afternoon, Charles, he came wandering into my library and told me all about it. I gave him directions back there, where he said that he'd seen the girl. And that's probably exactly where they both are right now."

"I don't know whether I believe this or not, Miss Alice. I don't know whether I want to believe it."

"That's the most honest remark I've heard from a clergyman in some time."

"You should come to church more often, then."

"Touché. Charles, you do me good. Maybe I will come to church."

"I'll look for you. . . . I think Emily is someone else I should talk to about this."

"I'm surprised she hasn't sought you out already."

"She may be embarrassed to."

"Silly girl," Miss Alice said.

"Emily," the preacher said, "is one of God's holy fools."

Mr. Gilchrist had a long conversation with Emily. More accurately, he spent a long time on the telephone, during which she did much of the talking and he said "Mm-hm," or "I see." After she had hung up, he sat in thought for a while. Either one of his congregation was deeply troubled, or something that might trouble everyone was at work. He would have to watch. He always watched his congregation anyway, just as Miss Alice watched her library patrons. Sometimes people fell asleep in the back rows during his sermon. And the front rows too. And if truth were told, that happened more often than sometimes. But physical rest, spiritual rest, whatever they needed, it was all right.

No, people would talk about anything. That was no news to him. He didn't believe that this furor over something untoward at that old house would bring more people into his church. Nor did he believe it was of Satan, which was just an excuse, a simplistic camouflage for the things people did to each other.

The girl Ashgrove Frazier had been abandoned by her father, neglected and misunderstood by her mother, and spoiled rotten by her grandfather.

Mr. Gilchrist thought of Francie Lee Frazier, who had left for parts unknown as soon as she decently could. He remembered something of the unhappy wrangles between Ashgrove and her mother.

I could write to Francie Lee, I suppose, he thought. Howard Yeargin might have her address. But what would

I say? Madam, come exorcise your daughter? Undo whatever it was that you did?

No, nothing would ever be as easy as that.

Ginny Reynolds had tried to call Redfern back, a few times; she hung on to the receiver with sweaty palms and listened to the switching of the long-distance circuits, trying to make the connection, dwindling into nothing. Sometimes his phone was busy. Other times there was no answer. Finally she knew that she would not try again, but when she asked herself why, she got different answers; inertia, horror, or pride.

When she asked herself how she and Redfern had got in this fix to begin with, she got different answers too. Carelessness. Embarrassment. Fear of taking the pill. Maybe she just wanted to be Redfern's mother; he was easier to get along with when you placated him. She had known him since she was six and he was four; he had been a difficult and charming little boy and he was still difficult and charming.

Maybe she just wanted to be anyone's mother.

Well, it certainly looked as if she was going to be, if she didn't do something, and she hadn't yet done anything.

The people in her office were understanding. Perhaps they hoped that she'd come to her senses and give the baby away, but they needed her too badly to put much pressure on her. She was all right for money thus far. And her family in Norfolk would help her. They would prefer that she not come home, but they would help her, rather than have their first grandchild thrown down the drain or given away.

It would be a lot simpler if I'd get rid of it before it's too late, she told herself. I could call the abortion clinic myself; I sure don't need Redfern for that.

It already is too late. I always said if this happened I'd go ahead with it, and it has and I am.

And it would not be a lot simpler anyway, not for me.

She was not deceived; she was acting, or failing to act, not out of conscience, but from sheer driving ego. The child was hers; Redfern had given it up. What he didn't want, she refused to destroy.

The ego is stronger than the conscience, any day.

Ginny lived in the northeast corner of an old mansion, built in a style unkindly known as Grover Cleveland Gothic. Her kitchen, through which you entered, had been the butler's pantry, her bedroom had been the kitchen, and her living room had been the dining room. Part of the dining room. The other part was now included in the next apartment. Left for Ginny was one large, ornately tiled, and heavily manteled fireplace, one stained-glass window—Tiffany roses—surmounting it, and one clear-glass window to the right of it. The room resembled a cave, but at least it was cool. With its high ceiling it rarely went above seventy in there, as the landlady, Mrs. Franklin, who lived in the sunny half of the house, was fond of remarking.

Mrs. Franklin was a great cook. She served heavily spiced and seasoned meals to old Mr. Franklin, who must have an iron-clad digestion. For some time Ginny had amused herself sorting out the flavors of pot roasts and fricassees—tomato, onion, bay leaf, thyme—but lately the odors of cooking sickened her, and she lived mostly on instant broth, soda crackers, and vitamin tablets.

Mrs. Franklin was also intensely religious. She could often—as now—be heard singing that to the old rugged cross she would ever be true, its shame and reproach gladly bear.

This still might not be such a bad place to keep a baby.

He or she would enjoy the reds and blues and purples of that colored window. He—or she. Ginny put her hand to her side, as she had seen other pregnant women do. She knew *it* was there, but it didn't know *she* was.

The *Aegis* ran one facetious piece about an alleged haunted house, but no more. After a stern phone call from Howard, and a mild one from Mr. Gilchrist, it went back to reporting overgrown garden vegetables, marijuana hauls, still busts, and high-school football games.

# 6

THERE NOW BEGAN what Ashgrove declared to be a siege. She and Martin were interrupted over and over by visitors from Masonborough and environs. They collected whatever they valued that could readily be moved and carried it all to the barn. This included a selection of books, the deck of cards, candles and matches, as well as the cat family and the guitar; they made several trips with the kittens and Trilby, who strenuously disliked being moved.

"Everybody and his extended family has been out here," Martin said. That might not have been true, but it certainly seemed true at the time.

He disliked the notion of keeping his guitar in the barn, which was dusty and cobweb-crusted to a degree he had never before experienced, but the only other choice seemed to be one of the chicken houses.

"You could leave it outside," Ashgrove suggested. "It might rain then. Murphy's Law, you know. We do need rain."

"If Murphy's Law is the one I'm thinking about, I know all about it. And we don't need rain that bad. What are you taking those candles and matches for? Do you want to burn the place down?"

"I'm going to sit outside with them. I might need to read."

At some point during the siege, they discovered what Howard Yeargin had imposed upon them. Ashgrove threw the FOR SALE OR RENT sign down in the grass.

"There must be some way to get these lockboxes off," she said, "but I can't figure it."

"Can't you?"

"Can you?"

"It's not hard."

"Well, help me."

"Just leave them alone for a while. If we have to get in, we'll get in."

"I guess we can endure out here, for a while."

She came to hope and believe that the less trouble she made, the sooner everyone would go away and let her back in. So they were stuck with the barn, which had its own atmosphere, but not an unpleasant one. The heavy smells of silage and the ammoniac leavings of cattle had blended into a warm darkness, shot with vague sunlight that was burdened with dust.

Martin had not seen many barns in his time, but he figured, if you'd seen one, you'd seen 'em all. In his first days on Ashgrove's place, he had not taken time to explore the back lot. Now that he was here, it looked run-down, countrified, and innocuous. The barn, silo, and sheds had been white once, shingled with gray. Rank grass and weeds shot up against their peeling sides: cockleburs, powerful-smelling catnip, and pokeweed with a rich-looking crop of inedible berries. The only color came from the red pokeweed stems and the heavy heads of bloom on the crape-myrtle bush; they were of a watermelon pink that was almost too bright to take.

Most of the large and valuable farm equipment had been sold off or taken away. What was left in the barn and other sheds had not been thought worth removing: old hand tools, bits of leather and scrap iron, chipped cider jugs and mason jars, and stacks of defunct magazines. He had a notion that some of these things, if reamed out, might be still in demand by those who would buy anything and call it an antique.

There was one last shed. It was too big for a chicken house and too small for a barn; he wondered if it could have once housed a light plant or electric generator of some sort. It was locked, but the hasps were falling out of the wood, and the doors opened with one sharp pull.

What reared up before him had the unexpected appeal that is sometimes found in the totally ugly. Its great round boiler carried excrescences of a big cylinder like a grasshopper's leg and a big driving wheel. It perched on other wheels that were high and skinny-spoked and black, and its tall stack was topped with a scalloped strainer. It was an old-fashioned steam-driven traction engine of the kind that is almost never seen any more.

He knew where he had seen one: in the Smithsonian in Washington, beautifully done up in shiny black with red trim. You could drive by on Constitution Avenue late at night and see it all lit up behind a plate-glass window. But that one was meant to be drawn by a team of horses, pulled from farm to farm to run the threshing rigs. He hoped this one was different, but there was no way of telling till he got a better look.

He went around behind it and threw all his strength into a shove, but it would not move.

He leaned against the curve of the rear wheel and yelled for Ashgrove.

She was evidently not far off, for she came running, took in the scene, and said, "Mercy."

"Did you know this was here?"

"Yes, but I'd sort of forgotten about it. It isn't much use to me."

"Then what use is it? Can it run?"

"It was my grandfather's toy in his old age. He got it from someone he knew down at Berryville. He loved it. He thought he might make an auxiliary electric generator for us to use during ice storms and other disasters, but he never got to. He used to drive it in parades, though, whenever he got the chance. And fairs. All the threshermen and steam buffs would get together, from here to the Blue Ridge and all up and down the Valley. You wouldn't believe the scene. I suppose you think my grandfather was a real madman. . . . Well, he was, but I liked him. . . . I wasn't as attached to this thing as he was. It's a noisy, dirty old hulk, and a real beast to handle."

"That would figure. But it did run when your grandfather was alive. And it's self-propelled."

"Oh, yes. It's geared up somehow so you can drive it."

"Could *you* drive it?"

"Oh, no. I can't even drive a car. I never learned; I was petrified."

"Oh, God," Martin said, but not with any great annoyance. "How can I get it out of this shed?"

"I don't know. *He* used to use a tractor to tow it out before it got steam up. Needless to say, you can't get steam up in there, so you're kind of up the creek."

"Well, come on back in here and help me."

After several strenuous minutes, Martin said, "Why can't you get steam up in here?"

"The smoke would inconvenience you considerably."

"It wouldn't inconvenience me."

"I see your point. I do indeed. Do you know how to get steam up?"

"No. You're going to have to tell me."

"Oh, Martin. Whatever for?"

"Because I want to. I haven't wanted to do too many things lately, but I want to do this. And you've got to help me."

"I don't know anything about internal-combustion engines."

"Oh, God," Martin said helplessly. "This isn't one."

"You sure could've fooled me. What's all that boiler then?"

"See this cylinder here? Well, in an automobile engine, the combustion that drives the piston takes place in the cylinder itself, whereas in this case it takes place in this big old boiler, which is one reason why you don't see too many steam cars or other engines like this around any more. See?"

Ashgrove said that she saw.

"All right. You understand that much. This end is the smoke box—that's what they call it—and this end is the firebox." In both of them something had been making a nest—mouse, bird, or owl unspecified. "These front wheels are geared to the steering wheel. The cylinder is connected up to the rear wheels. You can stand on this little step behind the boiler and steer it, if you can stand the heat. I guess I can stand the heat. Now what I want you to do is tell me everything you can remember about how your grandfather ran this thing."

"But why? Why?"

"I'll think of something once I get it running."

"The Story of Mankind," Ashgrove said. "Well, if Ray Charles drives a car and can't even see, I don't know why you can't drive a steam engine, whether people can see you or not."

"How would you know if Ray Charles drives a car?"

"I seem to recall I read it in *Playboy*. One of Jake's."

The first thing Ashgrove said they had to do was fill the boiler. It took hours. They didn't get tired, but they got horribly bored.

"We must've carried ninety-seven buckets of water."

"That's the origin of the phrase 'Old Ninety-Seven.' "

"That doesn't have anything to do with it. That was a railroad engine, this is a farm engine."

"It's still a good song."

"Yes, it is."

They began singing, to break the monotony.

*"It's a mighty rough road from Lynchburg to Danville
And lyin' on a three-mile grade."*

"I didn't know you knew that song."

"Everybody knows that song. Fine old bluegrass sound."

"My grandfather told me that was one of the most popular records Victor ever made."

"That sure tells us something or other about the taste of the American public," Martin said, remembering Miss Alice, and tickled by Ashgrove's casual use of "Victor" when everyone knew you were supposed to say RCA.

"Francie Lee threw our records out. I stood there wringing my hands, but I couldn't stop her. I had nothing to play them on anyway, but there were some real goodies."

"I can imagine."

"I bet you can't. We had 'The Wreck of the Shenando-ah' backed with 'The Death of Floyd Collins.' Most mournful things you ever heard. Went like this."

"No, don't bother. Don't sing it." Still, the very awfulness of Ashgrove's songs had a dubious charisma. "I'm going to go take a break."

"You want to play some I Doubt It?"

"I don't know."

"Just because you doubted me all the time and ended up with half the deck."

"Just because you don't ever lie."

"Oh, I lied. You just have trouble telling when."

The next step was cleaning the flues, which were in the front end of the boiler behind an iron door with FARQUHAR stenciled on it. "Well, farq you," Martin said grimly at one point. The flues were no easy job to clean, being crusted with soot, creosote, miscellaneous droppings, and other residual effluvia left over from burning wood. They did the best they could, using rags and a worn-out brush they had found tucked in among the outside piping.

"All right, now what?" Martin said.

"Well, it sounds crazy, but my grandfather used to start getting the fire up and then oil the engine while he was doing it. Everything seemed to percolate together better that way."

"This is like in science fiction, where there's this decadent race who don't understand their own machines."

"And then along comes someone who's different,"

Ashgrove agreed. "I wonder where the oilcan is. I suppose we could use candle grease if we had to."

They went off to the woodpile, the first of several trips. They kindled a fire and began feeding it slowly. It took about two fretful, suspense-fraught hours before the steam gauge registered any pressure. At Ashgrove's cautious instructions, they watched the pressure rise and opened the draft. Smoke mounted and clouded in the confined space of the shed.

"Just think how dirty we'd be, if we could get dirty."

"Just think how asphyxiated we'd be, if we could asphyxiate."

They did not have to grease with candle tallow after all. The necessary oilcan had been sitting on a rafter of the shed. Martin oiled any holes and bearings that seemed to need it. He went around tightening loose bolts, using a wrench where he could and main strength where he could not. It was hard to see what he was doing, and everything was finally happening faster than he had expected.

"How is that pressure? Is it up enough?"

"I think so. I wouldn't put much more than a hundred pounds; it might not be safe."

"Well, that's close enough for government work. Are you ready?"

"You drive her, and I'll stand right here."

"Decadent."

"I just want to watch."

"Why is it all right for you to stand and watch and it's not all right for me to?"

"I never said it wasn't all right for you to."

"Yes, you did, and you called me a scandalmonger."

"Things were different then."

"They're different now too."

"Yes, aren't they?"

"Well, decadent one, tell me now, how do you take off the brake? I can't seem to figure it out."

"You don't take it off. That's one thing I do know. She has no brakes. You close the throttle when you want to stop, or throw her in reverse when you're going fast."

"Oh, God," Martin said. He put the engine in gear, rolled it back and forth a few times to get the grease perking right, and drove blasting and clattering out of the shed, into the pale light of what had been a quiet afternoon. Ashgrove cheered, inaudibly. There weren't many places he could go from here, except the lane to the county road and the field track to the railroad. He warped it around the barnyard a few times. "I thought this thing would steer like a Sherman tank. I was wrong. It steers like two Sherman tanks." Then he closed the throttle and it rocked to a noisy halt, standing there like a time traveler from the dawn of the industrial revolution, ugly and sullen and full of an indescribable, far-out charm.

"Now what, young hero?"

"Wait till it's good and dark and take it somewhere."

"I suppose you know it can't go very fast or very far. Not more than three-four-five miles an hour, and you have to throw on wood every so often."

"I had thought of that."

"You can't get away if anyone tries to chase you."

"Let them be the ones to get away."

"I envision them crawling along in some sort of weird awestruck motorcade."

"Unsafe at any speed."

"I don't think I've ever seen you so amused."

"I don't amuse easy."

He jumped down and began chocking the wheels and regretfully damping the fire. Still, they had plenty of wood and water; it would be little trouble to get steam up again. Ashgrove said pensively, "Way down yonder in the middle of the field, Angel workin' at the chariot wheel."

"Quiet."

"Excuse me."

The days were getting shorter all the time, but it seemed like a long while until dark. Ashgrove left Martin wiping and greasing and went up to the house to water her plants. It had been hot all day, and still no rain, though dirty smears of heat lightning pulsed and flickered beyond the hills to the west.

For once, she had not heard the car drive up. Staying farther away from the road took care of that. But here came Emily Yeargin, uneasily picking her way around the side of the house through the grass and the Spanish needles.

It was too late for Ashgrove to run, though she would have liked to. She set down the watering can beside the pump and flattened against the kitchen door, waiting to see what Emily would do.

"Ashgrove, that is you, isn't it? . . . Ashgrove. . . . Is there any way I can help you?"

Go away, Ashgrove mouthed silently. She nearly said it aloud, but thought it best not to encourage conversation. She sensed an almost frightening pressure from this intense little lady. That's silly, she thought. *She's* supposed to be scared of *me*. Ashgrove had lately felt compassion for no one but Martin Evans, and not terribly much of that, but now, as well as disturbance, she felt concern for Emily.

"What do you want?" Emily insisted. "What will put you at rest? I thought ghosts were always after something, and if they got it, they didn't bother you any more."

That was too much to be ignored. Ashgrove opened her

mouth to demand, "Who's bothering whom?" Just at that moment a rhythmic noise began, beyond the house, beyond the hedge. It sounded like a giant pounding on the other side of the sky. Looking at that sullen sky, you might almost believe such a thing.

"Oh, my God, what's that?" Emily gasped.

Ashgrove knew. "It's Martin splitting kindling," she said. "Him and his engine." Emily did not stay to hear this. She broke and ran, stumbling back to her car in the gathering darkness.

Ashgrove went back and found Martin. She said, "Did you hear any of that? It was your friend, the blond lady. You scared her off, axing. It was right scary. I felt sorry for her. But then again, you know, she's sort of a good person."

"What do you mean, a good person?"

"Well, I mean, I get the feeling, if she saw Oedipus Rex with his eyes running down his face, she would say, 'Can I help you?'"

"And what would you do, if you saw Oedipus Rex with his eyes running down his face?"

"Oh, well. Scream *argh* and run off, I guess."

"That figures."

"Well, what would *you* do?"

"I will decide that when the time actually comes."

"You'd just pretend you didn't notice anything. Oh, I don't know! I don't know any more who ought to be scared of whom, or sorry for whom. She wasn't scared of me. She wanted to help me. She was just scared of what she didn't understand. Anyway, I hate to admit it, but you were right. My house is threatened. There are so many people, and there's only one of me."

"Well, you can always leave. They can't hinder you from that."

"Hinder me? I don't know where I'd go."

"Anywhere. Anywhere at all."

"I'm only interested in right here."

"Well, would you be interested in taking a ride away from right here, if it weren't permanent, or anything serious like that?"

"Oh, yes. Let's take it around to see Jake. He'd adore it."

"All right." Martin said slowly, dropping his sarcastic tone. "Let's go see Jake."

The ten-o'clock train had long gone by. They had played several hands of I Doubt It and a couple more of gin rummy while they waited to get steam up. The gibbous moon was nearly halfway up the sky. It was at that stage in its northern journey when it crossed the sun's waning toward the south.

"You sure can't take a notion to just jump on and ride off with one of these things."

"It sounds like Grandma's pressure cooker."

"It does not. It sounds like the *African Queen*."

"You watch too many movies. That's decadent."

"Are you going to watch this time, or get on?"

"Oh, I'll get on."

There was hardly room for them both side by side on the step.

"Let's hear how the whistle sounds."

EEEEEK.

"Now that sounds like Grandma's teakettle."

The great iron wheels lurched down the lane. The one big cylinder banged and shuddered, rocking the engine with every stroke. Steam, working or wasted, sighed and gasped. Heavy fragrant woodsmoke piled out of the stack. They careened down Ashgrove's road at five crashing miles an hour.

Jake Galey was asleep and dreaming. He thought he was a little boy in St. Croix Falls during the war. The trains used to run all night long, between the Twin Cities and Duluth; the steam-powered switch engines and freight locomotives shrieked and chugged and shunted constantly. One of them had arrived right under his window. He rubbed his eyes, felt of his beard, and realized that he was no longer a little boy, but that under his window there was still something extremely noisy. Some voices were also to be heard singing, with more enthusiasm than skill, that old song about when we hit that White Oak Mountain.

If those drunks want their muffler fixed, it's beyond me. They'll have to get home the best way they can.

The noisy engine was not retreating. He suddenly remembered the last time he had heard something like it—old Mr. Frazier's steam tractor—and he said, "Jesus God."

"Jake! Do wake up! I didn't think you'd be asleep," shouted a familiar voice from below.

"It's after midnight," Jake yelled back.

"It's supposed to be. We didn't want to take this thing on the road otherwise. Afraid someone might try to chase us. Can't you just picture it?"

"Well, did you just want to show me your granddad's toy, or was there something more important?"

"Well, yes, there was. We needed to talk to you."

"Come on up then," Jake said.

There was a brief delay, which involved blocking the wheels and banking the fire, which had better not be allowed to go out. Jake pulled on some grubby work pants over his underwear. Then he switched on the bare bulb that lit his room. The visitors came up quietly and sat down on the floor with their backs against one of the board-and-cinderblock bookcases.

So there really were two of them now; Ashgrove hadn't made up her story. The boy whom Jake had only seen lying ruined and wasted under an army blanket by the side of the road had in some way come back and stayed.

Was there ever going to be any end to this? Who else was going to come to people his room? Why not Keats, Nathanael West, Mozart, or Sylvia Plath? What about the numberless and nameless dead of this whole part of the world? No, any more would be too much to take. He was outnumbered even now. He didn't understand why he didn't run screaming into the night, but the two of them looked more harmless than not, sitting there quietly, pale, throwing no shadow in the harsh light. What trouble could they bring with them? What could they do to him? Enough had already been done to them. There was his old friend Ashgrove, diminutive and shock-haired as ever. She seemed exhausted and nervous but at the same time extremely pleased. The most noticeable thing about Martin was the strong grip that he had on himself. He was watching everything and saying nothing. He had severe blue eyes that were taking everything in and trying to make sense of it. He still looked like forty miles of bad road. Whatever his real age, he didn't look old.

"Hi," Jake said, and sat down heavily on his bed.

"Hi," Martin answered.

Ashgrove introduced them, though each of them already knew the other one's name. She said, "I've been wanting you all to meet forever."

Jake said, "Well, tell me what brings you up here, other than Mr. Frazier's steam engine."

"Wasn't that fantastic? Martin discovered it and took a notion he was going to fix it, so that's what he did."

"Wasn't it in awful bad shape?"

"No," Martin said. "It really wasn't too bad. I was lucky. It idles pretty rough," he added. Then he seemed to think better of having said even that much and was quiet again.

"Really, Jake, the problem is this. What's going on with my house? I thought you might be the one to know."

"What's going on? What isn't going on? You've become folklore. People are always driving in here and asking me about it. I tell them I don't know anything."

"Thanks."

"Here, you can look at these papers. There was something in the *Aegis* last week, but there hasn't been anything since. There are some copies of the *Post* over here too. You can see them if you want, but of course they don't tell anything about haunted houses. Other than the White House."

Martin immediately took cover behind a week-old section of the Washington *Post*.

"Oh, for pity's sake," Ashgrove said. "Ratsbane. So they really want to sell it. . . . Booo. . . . And they're having trouble. . . . Yay. . . . Isn't there anything that can be done? Can't it just stay like it is? Empty and haunted?"

"Apparently not."

"Oh, woe is me, for I am undone."

"Your mother finally got the wheels rolling and turned it over to this realty man Yeargin to sell for her. I don't know him. He's evidently very successful, though; has developed a lot of the new parts of Masonborough. I gather most of your surrounding acreage is being leased to other farmers around here, for the time being."

"That's all right; I don't mind that; I'm glad they'll be using it. But I don't want someone to use my house."

"I suggest you guys go off and find another empty house that isn't so conspicuous. There are plenty in the District, for instance."

Ashgrove's face set stubbornly. "I don't want an empty

house in the horrible District. I want mine. I went through quite an ordeal to get that house, and I'm staying in it."

There was a short interlude, during which Martin put down the paper. She raised her fist to her mouth, seeming to realize that she had said more than she ought. Jake decided to say nothing, the situation being better left unstressed.

She added, "Lovely we're having weather, isn't it?"

Martin leaned forward and wrapped his arms around his knees. His sharp, serious face took on a look of interest. "She's got a point. The District is a graveyard."

"Parts of it are okay," Jake said.

"Not the parts with all those empty houses."

"No."

"Bad news. I'd rather be gone to some other place."

"California," Ashgrove said flatly.

"That or somewhere."

They both seemed to relapse into their own thoughts.

"Or there's another thing," Jake said. He was just talking to hear himself talk and ease the vague tension. "You could pretend to go away, be exorcised or whatever, and then after the house was sold and people had moved in, you could reappear. It wouldn't be too honest, but at this stage of the game I doubt that it matters."

"I never thought of that. That's a grand idea. We could be ghosts in residence. Suppose there were children. I could read to them."

Martin gave her a skeptical look. "Maybe you can see yourself doing that, but I can't. They can't see us, and they'll crack up. I don't want any part of that. I would rather leave."

"Leave, then," she advised.

Jake said, "I can see you, and I haven't cracked up."

Martin said, "Miss Kinsolving in the library saw me and didn't crack up. Seemed pretty rational, in fact."

"Oh! Miss Alice!" Ashgrove said. "I'm scared to death of her."

"You ought not to be," Martin said.

"That's quite some lady, Miss Alice," Jake said.

Ashgrove fidgeted.

"However," Jake went on. "It does seem that when ghosts have to share houses with people, they tend to turn into poltergeists, or anyway the people think they do."

"Oh!" Ashgrove cried. "Poltergeists! Scum of the earth! Crumbs! Lowest of the low! I'm a person, not a noise."

Jake said, "Ghosts are supposed to be inarticulate creatures, staring at you in silent, agonized appeal, and I get the fifty-thousand watt voice of Virginia."

He noticed that Martin was quietly laughing, but Ashgrove said, "Agonized appeal, yes. Silent, no. Anyway, Jake, in spite of everything, it's been nice knowing you."

"Well, I'd really hate for you to leave. I hate to change neighbors. No telling what kind of weirdos you will get."

"You just never do know," Ashgrove agreed.

"What I will do is, I'll ask around in town; I'll even call Howard Yeargin's office and see if I can find out anything and what you can expect."

"Would you? That would be so helpful. You just don't know how fatiguing all this rumor business has been."

"Speaking of fatigue . . .," Jake said.

"I guess we were rude to come barging over at this hour of the night, except that we're sort of disoriented about time."

"It's all right. Tomorrow's Sunday."

"Is it? You could've fooled me. The cocks are crowing on merry middle-earth, 'tis time we were away."

"You know, Ashgrove, if you didn't think you were some figure out of balladry, you'd get along a hell of a lot better."

"Everybody has to think of themselves as something," Ashgrove said.

"Maybe you're right," Jake said. "Maybe everybody does. While we're on the subject, I'm going to have a nightcap."

"What of? Not that dandelion swill?"

Martin closed his eyes and kept his face expressionless. He knew that even if he had a drink in his hand he couldn't drink it, but still he would have liked to have one, even perhaps dandelion swill. Jake got two glasses that had once held jelly and a green bottle that still held brandy. He handed one slosh to Martin and took one himself. Ashgrove took nothing.

"Oh, God," Martin said in place of thanks.

He had first learned to drink brandy for sore throat and toothache. Then he had really learned to appreciate how it burned its way down, even cheap brandy, which this wasn't. He could almost, though not quite, remember how good and scalding it would feel. Martin, like most people he knew, had tried various methods to make himself feel good, comforted, or oblivious. And unlike many people, he still thought that liquor was best and brandy was best of all.

Born in corruption and raised in glory.

He began to understand why Ashgrove thought so highly of Jake.

"Can we have some music?" she was asking.

"Sure," Jake said. "What do you want?"

Martin did not care. Anything would suit him. He had been making his own music for days now—whatever music there was, he and Ashgrove had made it—but he could not remember the last time he had heard any recorded music, which was a thing he had always taken for granted before.

Ashgrove and Jake went through albums, quarreling amiably. He said that for an atheist, she sure liked religious music. She said that for religious people, some of those composers were pretty darn good.

Martin had no idea what time it was now. Probably near daybreak. He hoped the engine hadn't gotten cold. Ashgrove had got up a couple times to turn the records over. They had listened to cosmic, operatic liturgy, close harmony of those in extremity of desperation; it was like cosmic movie music from those days when being taken to the movies was a transcendent experience, the soprano crying *"Libera me"* and the contralto declaring *"Alle Lust will Ewigkeit."*

Ashgrove whispered, "That's a very nice contralto piece. If you happen to be a very nice contralto."

He closed her mouth with one finger. "Sh."

She edged her shoulder closer to him. "Can you understand any of it?"

"Enough."

Jake was asleep. He snored slightly but not overpoweringly. Ashgrove had pulled the sheet up over him. Martin got to his feet, feeling that he ought to be stiff, but he was not. He said, "Oh, my God."

"That's the most reverent tone I've ever heard you use."

"It's the most reverent I've felt in quite some time."

"We've got to go."

"I know."

"I'm afraid we'll wake Jake up."

"I wouldn't worry about it."

They started the engine, working as quickly as they could. It was still fairly hot. Evidently it couldn't cool off on that hot night. No lights came on upstairs. Before much longer they were lurching down the eastbound county road, which crossed the railroad tracks not far from Jake's. A train was coming, blowing for the crossing, which was guarded with electrical gates, this being the main line. Martin threw the reverse on and managed to halt his engine. In the fading darkness they could glimpse the train, northbound, its headlight swiveling frantically. Its glimmering silver sides were postered with red-and-blue Amtrak logos. The passengers would be in Washington in time for breakfast. Even if any of them were awake, they were traveling too fast to notice the odd machine waiting at the crossing.

"Mm," Ashgrove said.

"Mm," Martin said.

"The last car is always an anticlimax. There should be Harry Truman on the back platform, or something. Martin, did you ever think there was anything funny about this railroad track? I meant to ask Jake and I forgot."

"What could be funny? It's just a crummy old railroad track."

"Well, when the locomotive was coming—I always liked trains, I'm not afraid of them at all—but it gave me a kind of weird feeling, what they call *déjà vu*, you know? That's supposed to be French, but it's funny; it doesn't look like my idea of French when you write it down."

"Exactly what sort of weird feeling?"

"Expecting some kind of disaster. I've noticed it before. It's worse down at Frazier's Crossing. Do you know where that is? I guess I never showed you. It's off that way, south of here, on a field road."

"Number six hundred and forty-seven, Virginia Department of Highways."

"Oh, hush. We could go back that way. I want to show you."

"Not now. Let's go. I want to get this thing in before good daylight."

Ashgrove asked Martin if he ever felt like a troll, trying to get back to his lair before he turned to stone. He said not that he ever noticed. Then he shoved the engine in forward gear and they vibrated off, soon beginning to sing again about the mighty rough road from Lynchburg to Danville.

The steam engine was more trouble to run than anything Martin had ever owned or even heard of, but he was pleased with it nonetheless. Ashgrove helped him, when she was not busy with other things. They brought wood and water for it, and greased it as best they could. It used as much of everything as it could get.

They took to wandering farther afield, hiking the back roads in the daytime. Mason was a big, spread-out county, but most of its people now clustered near the county seat. Only here and there were little crossroad towns—hardly even towns, just a few scattered structures that might once have given a place a right to a name: little belfried country schools, long since closed; railway sidings and shuttered buildings; old filling stations, their concrete grown over with intransigent weeds, the round glass insignia shattered out of the rusty nine-foot pumps.

Occasionally they would meet small wild animals, scampering chipmunks and rabbits, lumbering wood-chucks and turtles. These creatures went about their business, neither shy nor forthcoming. The very colorings and markings that made them hard to see also made them beautiful, when you did see them.

Had there really been that many flowers the half-delirious day that Martin walked into Masonborough and back? Pink clover, blue chicory, white Queen Anne's lace, purple bitter nightshade, asters, goldenrod, orange-yellow touch-me-nots by little rocky streams that ran, drought-lessened, just barely audible under bridges and culverts. Those were the pretty ones. Then there were the ugly ones, taking over the waste: nettles and jimsonweed, mulleins and thistles.

As they walked through the overgrown roadsides, the crickets and locusts creaked without letup. Only after some time did Martin realize that they ought to quiet down when you came near and start up again after you had left. Then he wished he had never noticed that at all, but still he kept walking, getting a feel for the slate-gray roads of this brown-and-green country, about which Ashgrove would tell him all that she knew and some that she had made up.

At night he would run the engine, after making reasonably sure that it was late. It surged and thundered and made an awful racket. He loved running it. It was like him; it had come here by some unexpected chance and didn't really belong here. It belonged to some place bigger than the little hills and farms of the Virginia Piedmont: some place out in the grain belt. It would never get to those places. There was no way you could run it. It was bound to stay right where it was.

People still kept coming by the house to explore, on and off, though less and less frequently now. They found the house undisturbed. Ashgrove hoped that her patience and forbearance might at last pay off. Martin began keeping the engine down at the edge of the woods, behind the southern slope and well camouflaged.

Unobtrusively walking, they went back to visit Jake once or twice more. He said little and they said little. They felt somewhat better for being around him, but they couldn't tell how he felt.

Martin said that he did not think Frazier's Crossing was any weirder or more depressing than any other place he had been in lately.

They lived in the barn and on the roads like gypsies. Or somewhat like gypsies. It was always the same barn and the same roads. The days had the heat of summer and the dullness of autumn; the season of equinox struck an uneasy balance.

Howard was still talking on the phone in the kitchen, though it was after ten. Finally he hung up, came into their bedroom, and said, "Emily, this has gone on long enough."

She knew exactly what was on his mind, but she was almost too sleepy to argue. She laid down her book on the bedcover and tried to look obliging. "It's really distressing me too. We're going to have to do something."

"Great. Did you have any particular plan?"

"Well, I was thinking about something that would help both you and them."

"Them? You mean all the jackasses that keep calling me up?"

"The ghosts. Do you know the latest? People are saying that old Raeford Frazier has come back. They're saying he runs that old engine of his at night. More than one person has heard it. I know something is really wrong out there."

"Honey. You're really wrought up over this, aren't you? I can't believe it's good for you. You ought to get your mind on something else. Would you like to give a party, have some people over? Get Mary Grace to help you."

"You're sweet, Howard. . . . No, a party isn't what I want to have. I want to have a séance. You know, where you communicate with spirits."

"I know what it is, sure, and I think it's a ridiculous idea."

"Well, it's not exactly what I want to do; it's more what I think I ought to do."

"I can see it's gotten important to you. I shouldn't have let you get so occupied with it."

"No, it's all right. Maybe I needed something to get occupied with."

"Well, I'd hardly think this was it. What do you do? How are you going to do it?"

"Well, I've read a lot lately," Emily said vaguely and abstractedly. "I'm just going to try to get their attention, ask them what they're really after, and get it for them. Then maybe they'll leave."

Howard flung down beside her and removed one of her pillows. "Suppose you can't. Suppose they won't."

"I'm going to try."

"You're only going to try once. Then forget it. I'll wreck the place if I can't sell it, and I'll never sell it if this talk doesn't die down. I'm at the end of my patience." He reached up and snapped off the light.

For an impatient person, he certainly went to sleep easily. No, that was another way of being impatient. You don't mess around. You just click off and grab your eight hours. Jarred out of her good drowsy mood, Emily lay awake for a while, trying to set her thoughts in order.

Howard was sound asleep on his back, with his right arm flexed upward. Hoping to doze off, Emily turned on her left side. She took hold of his wrist and forearm and cradled his rough boney fist under her chin.

"Emily, do you really think this is wise?" Mr. Gilchrist asked.

"No, I don't. It's just something I have to do."

"For Jews demand signs, and Greeks seek wisdom," the

142

minister sighed. "I think I see." If Joan of Arc was anything like Emily, he could understand how those French noblemen must have felt.

"I sort of wanted to have you on my side," Emily said. "But not any of that hell stuff, you understand."

"I don't think there's anything in the Book of Church Order about this sort of thing."

"Oh! Don't bring the Book of Church Order, for heaven's sake! I mean, just come as yourself!"

"I'll be there, Emily. As myself."

"Charles?"

"Yes, Miss Alice."

"Have you been watching Emily Yeargin?"

"I watch everybody in my congregation. But yes, I have."

"She's worrying me."

"In what way?"

"She usually doesn't read anything but a little bit of light fiction, but she's checked out everything we have on the occult, ESP, and survival after death, and sent for more to Richmond and Charlottesville."

"That's her privilege. Isn't that what you ladies are there for? She'll probably boost your circulation considerably."

"Charles, something's going on, and I'm not being told. I thought you preachers were there for counseling."

"I'm not the one you should ask, Miss Alice. Ask Emily."

"I will indeed. I won't have a bit of trouble with Emily."

"Mason County Library."

"Miss Kinsolving, please."

"This is Miss Kinsolving."

143

Jake told her who he was. "You don't know me, but I've been in the library on and off. I live out on the county road near the old Frazier place."

"Oh, yes."

"Well, you've been hearing the talk, I'm sure."

"Oh, yes," Miss Alice repeated noncommittally.

"Perhaps you don't know that there's more to it than just talk." That would do for openers, he thought; it could mean anything.

He waited for her to say "Oh, yes" again, but instead she said, "Please explain yourself, Mr. Galey."

"Are you ready for this, Miss Kinsolving? The ghosts have actually been seen; I saw them."

"That doesn't surprise me."

"Then maybe it won't surprise you to hear that they were anxious to know what was in store for their house. Are people beginning to forget, or is it the calm before the storm? They said they need a liaison; I guess I'm it. I thought I'd ask you because—well, because you seem as though you might know what's going on." This was not the full truth, but he could not very well describe his visit with Martin and Ashgrove the other night. "I called Yeargin, the realty man, but he won't tell me anything."

"Well, I have an audience here now, Mr. Galey, but if you'll leave your number, I can call you later. If Howard Yeargin won't talk to you, I will."

Jake gave his number. He heard a click on the line. Perhaps he had been put on hold, perhaps someone in the library had picked up one of the other extensions. He said, not sure if anyone was there or not, "I ought to stay out of this, but I don't want anything else to go wrong."

"Mary Grace, I need to talk to you."

"Yes, ma'am. I need to talk to you too."

144

"I—Mr. Yeargin says—it's really too much—I hate to say it—but Mr. Mac at the supermarket says too—was that *beefheart* in the last meatloaf?"

"Yes, ma'am."

"That's what I thought. It's really too much. We just can't take it. Mr. Mac said you've been calling up and adding on to the grocery order. This has just got to stop."

"Well, it is. I'm leaving."

"Now, Mary Grace, I'm sure we can work something out . . . ."

"No, I'm leaving. I already decided. My baby writes me she's got on full scholarship now. She's doing good. Things are a little easier. I'm going to take time off and take a dietitian's course at the hospital so I can get a better job. My husband agrees with me. My other lady—my afternoon lady—needs me more than you do. She's got several little children. So I'm sorry, but I'm leaving."

Emily looked down helplessly.

"You don't have enough to do," Mary Grace went on. "You need something to keep you busy, so you won't worry with those haunts. And eat healthy food." She hung up her uniform and left, looking trim in an old McMullen dress.

Emily watched her go. Inside the house it was as cool and unreal as a movie theater. She turned the air-conditioning thermostat up to ninety degrees and flung up the front window. The last of the summer rushed in, smelling of dry grass, ivy, and rotting leaves, bringing dust, pollen, and sunlight, and a faint flavor of dampness somewhere. Sometime it might rain.

# 7

THE SIEGE SEEMED TO BE OVER, though you couldn't be sure. At least there was a break in the intrusions from outside. Ashgrove had come up from the barn lot to attend to the neglected garden, which had gotten far out of hand. Martin went with her. He found that he was singing to himself, an old song from an earlier and less complicated summer, about seventy-three men who sailed out of San Francisco Bay.

"Your mentality is straight out of the Top Forty," Ashgrove told him waspishly.

"Well, what about yours? English One-oh-one?"

"Make that Two-oh-one."

"Sold to the grubby lady with no shoes on."

He had brought something to read—a paperback copy,

rapidly coming unglued, of Robert Louis Stevenson's short stories—but he didn't feel like reading. He rolled over and put his face in the unkempt grass. It was heavy, coarse stuff, with long blades and tall, jointed stems. It was crabgrass, actually, but it was interesting. It lay tangled over and around itself like a plate of spaghetti.

He didn't exactly want anything to eat. Sometimes he could remember how food tasted and smelled, but other times not. This afternoon, as he lay in the grass, what came back to him was not steak and apple pie but cool raw carrots and hot baked potato brimming with butter and well salted and peppered. These things made themselves of the earth and when they were dug out they brought something of it with them: its coolness and wholesome cleanness.

Ants were crawling on the blades of crabgrass like motorists on a freeway interchange. They were red ants, red as the Virginia clay that could be seen far down below the grass stems; it sparkled with mica, and was red as the Golden Gate.

No, not quite that red.

He turned on his back and stared at the sky, which was colorless and lent no color to anything else. At the very zenith showed a mottled patch of blue. This sort of sky was almost enough to make you believe, like those *Name of Science* people, that the earth could be a hollow sphere, inhabited on the inside. The bright-colored flowers of the back garden glowed like little alien suns.

On three sides they were closed in with privet hedge. The tall house blocked much of the fourth. The smell of grass and greenness was heavy and rank. From up high a dove called, and a bobwhite called from down low.

A tattered butterfly flapped by. It had been one of those black swallowtails with blue spots—a pretty thing—but

147

its wings were worn nearly to shreds, its swallowtails were no more. Martin remembered, from long-ago churchgoing days, how they told you that the butterfly was like the human soul. It cast off its wrinkled cocoon, spread out its beautiful wings, and flew away into the spring sunshine. What they didn't tell you was how the butterfly got to look at summer's end, and what became of it in winter.

All analogies broke down eventually, but that one more decidedly than most.

He said, "Ashgrove."

"I'm right here." She came and sat a few feet away from him.

"Are you going to stay right here forever?"

"I might. When's forever?"

"That's what nobody knows."

"I plan to stay here till I find out."

"You really don't ever think that you might leave?"

"What for?"

"There's plenty outside this hedge."

"Everything that's important to me is inside this hedge. Just about."

"You mean you're going to stay here till you or the house dissolves? Whichever comes first? I wonder which will come first. So we still exist because we had some energy left over. I'll buy that, but what does it mean? Suppose we last fifty or sixty more years and then vanish for good. Had you thought of that?"

"Yes, I had thought of it. Often. But I didn't know what to say, so I didn't say anything."

"Amazing."

"It may be that the gulfs will wash us down. . . . We might vanish for good, or we might not. There are supposed to be ghosts from other centuries, but I never met one to know it. They only seem to appear occasionally. Maybe they only exist occasionally. You and I exist all the time, except that time doesn't directly affect us. But the space that we're in is in time. That's what worries me about my house. What's going to happen to it? Ultimately?"

"One of several things. The house will be sold, and people will be able to ignore you and live happily ever after, or they won't be able to, and your house will be abandoned and fall apart."

"Oh, no."

"It certainly will. It's held together with spit and spackle as it is. You can't do all the repairs yourself, and you can't very well get anybody else out here to do them. Then there's a third alternative. They could tear it down, build a development or something."

"They can't do that!"

"Why not? They can do it easier than you can stay here forever, digging the garden, reading *Lord of the Rings*, making tea that you can't drink, for crying out loud, and playing with the cats."

"That's another thing. I can't leave my cats either. They'll become poor miserable strays."

"I bet Jake would look after them. He supports them single-handed as it is."

"He likes them."

"I didn't say he didn't."

"Well, I'm just going to have to think of something really drastic, and do it."

"If you hadn't done whatever it was in the first place, you'd still be alive and wouldn't have all these problems."

"And if you'd fastened your seat belt, young hero, you wouldn't be hanging around my place like a lost soul and I wouldn't have *any* problems."

"If I'm a lost soul, which I don't grant, what are you?"

"I'm not lost. I know where I am. I'm right here."

"Sure. Doing what? Waiting for the next accident to happen? Some other victim to show up?"

"Don't blame your bad luck on me. You were spoiling to get lost. Spoiling! What makes you so hateful?"

"*I'm* hateful?"

"Hateful! That's what I said! Hateful! You wrote the book. You came up off the road being hateful!"

"Well, I found myself in good company."

"Yes, I guess we deserve each other. . . . Why is that, do you suppose? Why do we carry on like this all the time?"

"Maybe it's how we know we exist."

"I already know I exist."

"Leaving aside all that, and whatever we did, and for whatever reason: Do you ever think what it would be like if we hadn't died?"

"Oh! I don't know. It grieves me sometimes."

"Suppose I'd decided to mess with using my seat belt for a change."

"Suppose I'd been living here—really living—and you happened to wreck your car, just slightly, not enough to hurt."

"I might still have come up and asked to use your phone. If I hadn't burst into flames first."

"No, I can't think about it. It's too confusing to think about."

"That's the Presbyterian coming out in you."

"Martin, what religion are you? You never told me. Not that it matters."

"I was raised Baptist."

"Well, you know how awful funerals are."

"I sure do."

"Well, at my grandfather's funeral, they sang this hymn that really got to me, as hymns do tend to do sometimes, even the bad ones. It went like this." She sang to him softly, a dreary little tune, old-fashioned sounding:

*"Our years are like the shadows*
*On sunny hills that lie*
*Or grasses in the meadows*
*That blossom but to die.*

"And I thought that was so sad. It got to me more than any of the Bible reading, or praying, or 'Rock of Ages' blasted out at top volume. For all the age my grandfather was, and his life was no more than that. It's not going to be that way with me. I'm going to stay here forever and ever, and watch the hills and meadows change, and change back again."

"Still, year after year. For how many years? Do you even know? When there are so many other things that you might do and places where you might be."

"But this is my place. I can't explain it to you. I didn't think I'd ever have to. I guess as time went by I thought you'd understand. It's home. It's just the way it looks and sounds and smells and the way it always comes back, day after day, year after year. I'll look out in the morning and see that tree, that field, those woods yonder, and remember how they looked last spring and how they're going to look this fall. I belong here. My grandfather left me this place and I love it better than anyone else ever did. People don't love their houses like they ought to. Did you think that ghosts couldn't love?"

"No."

"We love as much as anyone, maybe more. I love my house. If anything happens to it, or I have to leave, I'll be destitute. And when the time comes that there are no more empty houses at all because the world is packed with people—or when the people blow themselves to smithereens—I don't know what any of us ghosts will do. We can't get hurt, but what will we do? Where will we *be?* I don't like to think about it."

"It's enough to make you go off and join Zero Population Growth."

"Oh, ha. You've already done your bit for Z.P.G. So have I, if it comes to that."

"How do you know I don't already have quite a number of children?"

"Well. Do you?"

"Not that I know of." When she glanced at him sharply, he said, "Well, that is the standard answer."

"Oh! All you do is make fun! You don't help me at all!"

"I'm trying to help you, but you don't pay any attention. . . . Who dealt this mess?"

"The Great Cardsharp in the Sky, I once heard someone say."

She stalked away, declaring that she had work to do.

Martin turned over and stared into the grass again. His memory showed him things he thought he had almost forgotten. He remembered California more clearly than he ever would have believed. He could even smell it in his mind—far down the San Francisco peninsula— eucalyptus, acrid, medicinal, and faintly tomcatty; chaparral with the scent of a handful of herbs. The wind came pounding in from the coast ranges with five thousand miles of the Pacific behind it. Inland, the peninsula had been raped flat to the ground and coffined in concrete, but in the hills and toward the coast it was still alive and wild. That part would be lost with the rest when the San Andreas let go, but while it lasted, here and there you would find a wasted, abandoned farm, marked by a

152

broken windmill and the stunted remains of an orchard. The half-ruined house would be narrow and flaking white, trimmed with carpenter work, built with a peaked roof to fend off snow that never came, by people who had come there from the northern states or the north countries of Europe. It would be shaded by gawky eucalyptus that rattled like dry bones, volatile as kerosine.

Of all that he had seen out there, why remember that?

He knew why; it was something that Ashgrove might approve of.

Why did he even care what she would approve or disapprove of?

He was not exactly sorry that he had met her. No telling what would have become of him without her; that was the brutal truth. He would never forget her either; there was no way he could forget her; he would always hear her in his mind, mocking him worse then he had ever mocked himself, and throwing at him an occasional farfetched compliment that was almost worse than mockery.

What would he ever do without her? The same as he would have done anyway.

He had to admire her stubbornness. He might as well admire it. There wasn't too much else he could do about it. Anyway, he had stubbornness of his own.

Strange how he could still smell eucalyptus, clean and astringent for all its acridity. There was nothing like that in Virginia. Virginia was still lush with honeysuckle, roses, and clematis, and the ripe-rank richness of heavy summer hung on and on. The bitter change to autumn had not yet begun. September was stagnant.

If it even was still September. But it probably was.

He was going to have to learn to tell time by the sun and the moon, the solstices and the equinoxes.

As the grayish day deepened into darkness, he went

after his guitar. Rather than enter the house again, he and Ashgrove were still grubbing around the back steps of the kitchen. Various cats squabbled and scuffled in the shrubbery. Ashgrove threatened to go get a screwdriver and remove all the lockboxes, but he told her she'd better not. To his surprise, she didn't. She seemed not to know exactly what else to do with herself.

"I wish it would rain," she said. "Oh, I wish it would rain."

"It's going to soon. It has to. Don't you feel the pressure?"

"Yes."

"It's weird; it's supposed to be low pressure."

"Yes. I feel it terribly anyway. It is weird."

Everything was a muted raincoat color, grayish-green except for the white flowers, which stood out almost unnaturally. Martin sang to himself, "Good night, you moonlight ladies, rockabye sweet baby James."

Ashgrove sat down on the bottom step. She said, "Maybe all music is a little night music—something people make for themselves in the dark out of splinters and string and bits of plumbing."

"How long did it take you to think that up?"

She replied quietly, "I've often thought it; I just never said it to anybody before."

A four-cylinder engine turned off the road and came chugging and clattering up the lane. The ignition quit and the parking brake set with a *grink*. "Son of a bitch," Martin said. "I'm so tired of all these damn invasions."

"That's Jake," Ashgrove said positively. For a few seconds she looked at Martin, who did not look back at her. Then she turned and ran down to meet Jake.

"Hi," she said.

"Hi," he said. "How's everything?"

"Fine, I guess."

"How's your friend Martin?"

"Raving and bitching. He's in a rotten mood."

"I don't blame him; I'd probably be too, in his case."

"No, you wouldn't. You'd do beautifully. You're not as high-strung as he is."

"Well, I don't want to argue about that. I've been thinking seriously. Why don't you guys get organized?"

"We *are* organized. At least as much as we need to be."

He closed a heavy hand on her wrist. Neither one of them flinched. "Ashgrove, you think that you're Zelda Fitzgerald, but you're going to turn into A Rose for Emily if you don't watch it."

"Is this a course in literature, or did you have something you really wanted to talk about?"

"I mean you better shape up and ship out." She laughed, but he went on. "Your friend has the right idea. You don't have much future here. Your past is here, all right, but not your future. He's right. He wants to leave. The only thing I can see keeping him here is you. And you ought to leave with him."

"I keep thinking, Jake. . . . If I don't leave, then he might come back, and I'd still be here, and he'd know right where to find me."

"That's an awful lot of conditions. And this is your Uncle Jake speaking, but people are more important than things."

Ashgrove thought of a poem. She said,

> "But she is early up and out,
> To trim the year or strip its bones;
> She has no time to stand about
> Talking of him in undertones."

"Every time I see you, Ashgrove, you get farther away, and stranger."

155

"I can't help it. I haven't done anything. Do you think I'm mad at you, or something? I'm not. You were good to come. Nobody else would have done it. But you'd better not stay."

"I know."

"Maybe all this is as it should be. You can't go on like this forever."

"That's what *I've* just been telling *you*."

"Well, I'm different; I *can* go on like this forever."

"Well, if you do decide to leave, I'll miss you."

"I'll miss you too."

He let go of her wrist and shoved his hands in his pockets. She took a few steps backward.

"Oh, Jake!" she said. "Great rooted blossomer."

"Write to me."

"But how will you write back? I'll read your book. Are you going to put me in it?"

"If I do, you won't recognize yourself."

"I didn't really love you," she said in a suddenly altered tone.

"It's all right. I didn't think you did."

"I just wanted to get that straight."

"Nothing is ever straight."

"The crooked straight, and the rough places plain."

"I knew you were going to say that."

"Oh, go away."

"Forgot I had something else to tell you."

"Oh, what?"

"There's going to be a séance; I have that from an unimpeachable source, namely Miss Alice Kinsolving. They're coming out here tomorrow night, probably with bell, book, candle, or God knows what."

"*Who* are coming?"

"Emily Yeargin, of course."

"As in A Rose for Emily?"

"Hardly. Emily, anyway, and I'm not sure who else. Miss Alice said she was coming herself, to lend sanity to the scene. They're going to try to communicate with you, and put you at rest. It seems to bug people that you're at large."

"Oh, ha. Nothing can put me at rest. It just isn't the sort of thing I do."

"Sometimes I think communicating isn't the sort of thing you do either. Plus which, you tell Martin that he's been heard running that engine of his. Only people think it's your grandfather, since there's no way they can tell it's Martin."

"Now that isn't funny."

"I'm sorry; I shouldn't have said anything."

"No, it's better to know."

"That's what I figured, so I drove on over here."

"Forearmed is forewarned."

"Knowledge is power."

"Well, I don't know what we can do that we wouldn't do anyway, but thanks for coming by; I really appreciate it."

"No trouble."

"Well, carry on, or whatever else you do in your spare time."

"Keep the faith."

He got into his car, turned it around, and headed it out. She lifted a hand to him and he returned the signal.

Martin was still sitting on the back steps where she had left him. She came up quietly. He paid her no attention. He was practicing a monotonous gospellike tune, which alluded to light come shining from the west down to the east. He was slapping it through the chord changes till it sounded bruised and weary.

He's like someone drowning, she thought, holding on to a piece of debris.

*But what am I doing that's any different?*

The world seemed to her to drop away around him as he sat there, his shoulders hunched over his fingerboard, his long legs cantilevered as if to balance the sound box. It had gotten much darker in the short time since she had left him. The set of his face was softened in the dimness. He was only a shadow among the shadows, and yet just then he was more real to her than anything else, and desperately beautiful, with a grim, understated, American Gothic beauty.

She just wanted to watch him.

He would tell her that that was decadent.

The urge to take care of him fought with the urge to squelch him.

She said, lightly and dryly, "What of the night?"

"What of it? Big deal. Happens every twenty-four hours."

*I've been squelched*, Ashgrove thought. She said, "Don't you want to know what that was all about?"

"You'll tell me anyway."

"You're not going to like this at all."

"Lay it on me."

"Well, that was Jake. He came to tell us about this séance that's going to be visited on us tomorrow night."

Martin swore.

"That's exactly right," Ashgrove agreed.

"I would've thought that they'd given up doing things like that."

"So would I. Evidently they haven't."

"Who dealt this mess?"

She was silent, watching him thoughtfully.

*This is where I came in*, he thought. *She's cheerful and I'm angry, though the reasons are different now. Or maybe even then they were the same underneath.*

He curbed his temper. It didn't matter. You couldn't attack this girl. She would either ignore you or give back as good as she got.

He said, "Ashgrove, you've been very nice to me."

Girls usually began looking troubled when you said this. She put her fists on her hips and said, "You better believe I have. I'm not often nice, either. I'm rude and ugly to most everyone."

"I'm not going to take much more of this, though."

"More of what? What have I done now? Other than usual."

"Nothing. It isn't you. It's just all these people, constantly coming in and out; it's the feeling of being in a goldfish bowl. That isn't all there is to it. But I don't need it. There's no way in the world you'll convince me that I need it."

"I don't need it either. I'm just going to endure till it's past and they've stopped coming. They'll stop, you know. People forget. Also, is all your work on the steam engine going to be for naught? You worked so hard on that, and I thought you liked it."

"The age of steam is over. Nostalgia is great, but enough is enough. Besides, it's just a big toy. You can go places without it better than you can with it."

"Go places? I believe you'd miss that tractor worse than you'd miss me. . . . You remind me of those people in the Soviet Union. . . . Are you really going to leave, not going to endure?"

"Sure I'm going to endure. Till Doomsday, or what. I'm just not planning to do all my enduring here. I'm not a hard-core Virginian like you."

"Did you think it was that? Being Virginian? Is that what you thought? But history isn't what matters to me. The country is full of history. Beautiful history, ugly history. For me, it's *this particular place. Itself.* No matter what it was named . . . Virginia . . . Transylvania . . . Slobovia . . . or the State of Panic . . . it's still *this place*. There isn't anywhere like it. Haven't you seen how beautiful it is?"

"Yes," Martin said. "And I'll grant you that, but have you seen West Virginia, or California, or all the places in between? I haven't. Not enough of them."

"But this is home."

"Ashgrove. Everyone has to move on from their home."

"But I just got here."

"I don't believe you're that different from everybody else. I don't believe you're that different from me."

"Oh! Maybe I'm not. I don't know what I am."

"I thought you did. I really thought you did."

"Not any more."

"If you keep looking back, you're going to turn into a pillar of salt." He hadn't known he was capable of going on like this. Possibly the Irish coming out in him, or the Baptist.

"No," Ashgrove said. "I don't have any more tears."

He got up and stood over her. She put out her hands to him. The night was heavy and far advanced. They fell into one another's arms. It was like falling into cold water, painful but cleansing and releasing. For all that she was so little and slight, she upheld him as much as he did her.

"Just hold me." Which of them said that?

"It's all right. I've got you."

They stood close, striving to get closer still. They had gotten past the horror, though there was always horror in closeness, just as there was in loneliness.

"I'm leaving. Not going to stay here."

"No."

"Come go with me."

"You finally asked that."

"I've been asking that the whole time."

"No, you just asked why I didn't leave."

"You love this place too much."

"It's hard."

"I know."

They swayed together, dropped to their knees, and overbalanced into the grass, where they lay crowded and tangled together. She turned desperately to him as the breadth of his shoulder pressed her down. He held on to her as if he both dreaded and loved her, as if she were part of the earth that bore him and claimed him but would never receive his seed. The searching cold dragged them together like strong current.

She said, "I'm going to get up."

"Go right ahead. I'll help you."

They knelt up and embraced again.

She said, "What am I going to do?"

"I'm not going to tell you what to do."

"Oh, you're not any help at all."

"I might say, Ashgrove, you're beyond help."

"We're not going to feel like this in the morning."

"No. It's too much to take." It was like zero weather when you touched something barehanded and froze to it.

"I've got to tell you something. I feel honor bound." She edged away, adding, "Now I don't know how to begin."

"Begin at the beginning; where else?"

"I can't tell where the beginning is. It's not so much what I did, but the way I began to feel about it. It might have been when you got here, or it might have been before that. Really, it was before that, but I didn't start to feel bad about it till afterward, after you got here, and I started to know you, and all." She put a fist to her mouth, incoherent with stress. "I'm trying to tell you what I did.. It's upsetting me."

"What you did about what?"

"Two years ago."

"Oh." He had guessed before that she had overdosed on something, but not on what, or why; it was beyond him.

"Well, I didn't want to leave. You must understand that."

"Yes."

"My grandfather died in early June. Two years ago. He went down in the woods to take out some timber. It's a part of the woods you don't know about. The man who was supposed to help him with the chain saw was late, so he went on anyway. He was impatient. And something went wrong; we don't know what; anyway, one of the trees fell on him."

"What kind of tree was it?"

"What in the world does it matter? It was a tulip tree."

"I'm sorry. That's awful."

"Yes. It was. By the time the man got there, it was too late, my grandfather was dying. I didn't even get to see him till they'd cleaned him up and put him in the coffin. He wasn't expecting to die, even though he was old. He expected that I'd be at least twenty-one when he did." She clenched her fists together and looked down on them.

"Ashgrove, you're getting yourself all bent out of shape, and whatever it is can't be that bad."

"Think not?"

"Surely not. Come on." She leaned her shoulder against him, but she would not look at him. They fidgeted around. Finally he got her settled down in the grass and jackknifed her against him, backward. She went on trying to tell her story.

"He left this place to me. I could have kept the house and the land around it, and with income from the other land I could have gone to college, some sort of college. Not that I'd've known what to do with myself. The

162

lawyers appointed my mother as the trustee, since she was my only relative. And she wanted us to leave—go somewhere more exciting. She looked on it as her chance to be independent. But I didn't want to leave. And she said I wasn't of age and couldn't stay here by myself, though I perfectly well could have. And we fought. We went around and around, screaming at each other, bursting into tears, the whole bit. I really wasn't quite in my right mind. I could see no end to it all. Do you know how it is when you can see no end to it all, when you don't think things will ever be different? You're older than me, but do you remember? So I decided if I got extremely sick and vomited she'd believe there was nothing I wasn't prepared to do to get what I wanted. . . . And maybe she would appreciate me a little bit more. . . . So I made a strong dose of jimsonweeds and drank it. And it stank, too."

He said blankly, "You can't mean that."

"You know what jimsonweeds are. Grow all around here. Kind of a corrupted petunia is what they are. Jimson-weeds, petunias, eggplants, tomatoes, and a lot of other stuff all belong to the nightshade family, only I didn't know that at the time. Everything I know about botany I taught myself after I died. So that was what happened. You have to watch that nightshade family. It's an atropine reaction and it attacks the nerves. Does it ever. Of course, it's a long haul to the hospital. My mother was lucky she didn't get tried for murder, actually, except if she'd meant to murder me, she'd have chosen some less conspicuous way, and everybody knew it. Actually I was much more abnormal than she was, and everybody knew that too. I wandered lonely as a cloud, if you know what I mean."

Martin did not say a word, nor move.

She went on, still facing away from him, and holding

163

one of his hands in both of hers, "I really should've told you this right from the beginning. Partly I didn't just to be ornery—partly because I hardly knew you—partly I just don't like to talk about it, because no one else can really understand. Then, as time went by and I got to know you, I was sorrier and sorrier; I realized it must make a pretty dumb story."

"I've done a lot of dumb things too. Some of them fairly recently." He was thinking of the train that he had casually allowed to run over him. Still, it wasn't the same. Or was it? He remembered the fear that things would never be any different, and the urge to turn toward anything to break the pattern. He also knew the desire for what Ashgrove called appreciation.

"I did the only thing I could think of, and it worked out all right, on the whole, because I've been here ever since, where I wanted to be. But telling you that—it would've been like complaining about the servant problem to somebody who doesn't even have food to put on the table. I realized that. I thought you'd get mad. You get mad so easily."

"The only thing is, there are ways to make yourself vomit that don't have such a permanent effect. Soapsuds, for instance."

"Well, suicide, unlike many other things, the better you are at it, the fewer chances you get to try."

"You hit big the first time."

"Right."

Time went by. They said nothing more. They did not need to. The words echoed in their minds.

I'm going to leave.

I know. But I'm going to stay here.

I know that too. You're going to stay here forever?

When's forever?

Nobody knows.

He forgot that he had ever wanted warm blood, warm breath, warm weight in his arms. He knew this girl and her strength and weakness as closely as he would ever know anyone, and she knew his. Whatever happened, that was true. He rested his face against her hair, which smelled like dozens of plain little plants with beautiful names. Indeed that was Ashgrove: a plain little creature with a beautiful name and qualities of refreshing and healing that might fade if she were uprooted.

Time went by. It was not day, but it was not really still night.

He said, "Ashgrove. . . . If you would still be here, I could come back again sometime." But she gave no answer; she had dropped asleep, a bundle of skinny arms and legs and roughened hair. Her face was almost hidden from him. He had never known her to sleep before. She had eased off so quietly. It would have worried him, but he figured that she needed the rest, having been wakeful for so long.

When he tried to lift her, she flinched and grasped out with her hands. So he left her lying on the ground.

The old house keys were still under the back steps. This was going to surprise someone or other. The realty people hadn't known that Ashgrove had these keys, and she hadn't known that she could use them. It was time now. He unlocked all the doors and took down all the lockboxes. It seemed like magic, but it was just human fallibility.

Anyway, locks were for honest people.

He went upstairs after one of the quilts and threw it over Ashgrove. Then he carried his guitar to the barn and set off to work on his plans for that day, and to get away by himself.

# 8

WELL ON IN THE DAY, Ashgrove came awake, still lying on the rough grass by the back steps. The sky was pale and threatening at the same time. She raised herself on her hands and stared around painfully. She was not used to sleeping, and it was hard on her.

"Oh, God," she said, pretending to be Martin, but that didn't make her feel any better. She added, "Ratsbane."

There was no one in sight, not Martin or anyone. The cats had probably given up on her. She pushed off the quilt—where had that come from?—folded it tenderly, and left it on the steps. The old Robert Louis Stevenson book was there on the steps too. Nothing was damaged, for it still had not rained. Then she realized that the lockbox had been taken down and was lying by the door. All of the lockboxes had been taken down. She carried them all down to the roadside and dropped them into the ditch.

"That's the first trash I've had on the place in quite some time," she said.

She pumped a bucket of water and went down to the barn to feed the cats. "You all don't have to be barn cats now," she told them. Martin's guitar was there, sheltered in its case. She carried it back to the house with her.

Then she went through the house flinging doors and windows wide open. "It's dirty in here; I need to clean." Nevertheless, she stepped outside again, through the front door. There was a lilac bush here in the front yard. It was old and large, but at this time of year it did not look like much; its arrowhead leaves were dim with dust. In April, though, it would be burdened with lilacs, and the damp air around it would be drenched with their scent.

In May, this place would be enclosed with rich honeysuckle fragrance. It smelled good now; the privet hedge was full of autumn clematis and the second blooming of the honeysuckle, but when the honeysuckle first bloomed, the hedge would be thickly tapestried with its white, cream, and orange, and you might as well not try to do anything but enjoy it for the time that it lasted.

Then afterward the privet itself would bloom, and the ligustrum-lucidum, which was some kin to it and to the lilac. Some people did not care for these heavy, cloying odors, but that was all right with Ashgrove. She liked them.

To every thing there is a season, and a time to every purpose under the heaven.

I really must break myself of quoting the Bible, but I don't think Ecclesiastes exactly counts.

Out back, the garden and the potted plants still looked neglected. She had not done enough work on them yesterday. The geraniums badly needed pinching. She knelt to attend to them. They were depleted, their leaves yellowing, but still sending up a few small fists of buds. The marigolds, petunias, and scarlet sage still bloomed valiantly; the orthogonal lavender and scraggly thyme still looked thrifty. Frost would not strike them for several more weeks. Fall drifted lingeringly into this part of the world, and after the flower colors were blackened, the leaf colors would smolder, blaze, and smolder till the end of November and beyond.

"In that garden of Elrond where none now walk," she said to herself. She was being Arwen Evenstar of Middle-Earth now. Away from the sardonic presences of Martin and Jake, she was free to ham it up as she liked.

She clasped her hands together. Then she decided that she had really better pull weeds. The weeds had gotten tall and straggling, but there were so many of them they looked rather showy. She fetched her bushel basket and filled it in a few minutes. For all their top growth, most of them seemed to have very little root system. Their job was to reproduce their kind, not to make roots. They would blossom, set seed, and die, leaving a myriad descendants for her to pull this time next year.

She emptied the bushel basket onto her compost heap and lay down full length in the grass. There were, predictably, weeds here, too: groundmint, clover, oxalis, even a hickory seedling. She gave a sharp jerk and it came up, still attached to its nut, whose shell was burst and malformed.

"Out of sweetness came forth strength," she said vaguely, and flung the seedling away. Then she scrambled up from the grass and glanced around her apprehensively, as though she were afraid she might miss something, as though something might have changed while her attention was distracted. She turned her eyes to the woods, where the hickories and tulip trees would soon be going up like pillars of smoky yellow flame, giving back to the gray autumn sky the light they had drawn from it all summer long.

All that day she could settle to nothing. It was awful. She weeded some more, leaving the beds in fairly presentable shape. She went for her broom and dustpan and a few vestigial rags and attacked the dust in the front part of the house. She put away the quilt in the kitchen cupboard. She fetched her other belongings that had been left in the barn, including the cards. She wiped the dust of the barn from under the guitar strings and put it back in its case, saying, "Though you can fret me, yet you cannot play upon me."

She needed to make some more candles, but she told herself she couldn't stand the ordeal. She was running out of grease anyway; it had been awhile since Jake had replenished her supply.

She tried practicing the piano, beginning with Chopin's Prelude in A Major, and missing the large chord in the twelfth measure, which was usual for her, since her fingers could hardly stretch an octave.

"God Almighty," said a severe voice in the back of her memory. "Try a sharp, would you please."

She said, "Ahhhhh." But she tried a sharp. That was better. She got the piece just about right the next time she played it.

There was no way that Hope or Mariana could be looking at her. Hope was bound and blindfolded like the Eight of Swords; Mariana's eyelids were half shut, gazing out of her moated grange. They were just pictures anyway. She took them down from the picture rail and turned them to the wall.

She dropped her voice an octave and tried a line from an old Melina Mercouri movie. "I gave you . . . meelk and honney. . . . In return you give me . . . poison." The role of Phaedra soon wearied her, however, and she abandoned it.

She turned to the Schubert piece called "Valse Sentimentale," which she had always liked, even though Martin made unmerciful fun of it. She didn't think it was as sentimental as all that. The syncopation saved it. Sentimentality meant overstatement; syncopation was leaving something unsaid, breaking the melody where you least expected it.

And I talk a lot, but I've still not said all that I might.

She got through the piece by pretending that the part with all the sharps was really written in D flat.

She fetched her garden book and looked it over. This was the third year now that she had kept records of when the various sorts of flowers bloomed, when she had repotted or fertilized, the extremes of temperature, and the gradual, day-by-day changes of spring and fall. It told her much that was not written in words.

She dealt the cards, but they told her nothing that made any sense.

She had waited a long time to get back into the house, but now she found that she could not stay in it. The heavy pressure from the sky was worse indoors. Breezes glimmered the leaves against the windows. She roamed out to the orchard, with its stunted slopes of trees gray-green-yellow like the sky. Rotting apples, spotted, streaked, and speckled, going to cider-pulp and to earth, trundled about underfoot. But overhead the boughs were as rich as Christmas still.

170

She loved the orchard, half derelict though it was. One thing she would have liked to bring with her from her past life was biting into a York or a Stayman, cold not from the icebox but from the bright air of October.

Any apple, no matter how warped and lumpy, when you cut it across the core, showed you the shadow of the blossom that it had once been. That was something: the five-petaled blossom and the dark star of the seeds.

Ashgrove sat in an apple tree all afternoon. Shy, nervous Pyracantha cat came and sat with her, but then retreated on some vague errand.

The wind rose. It began to grow dark. Pyracantha reappeared from wherever she had been and raised her anxious tiger face, looking to be fed. Ashgrove called her to the house and fed her. The other cats came too. They were nervous, and twitched their shoulders under their fur like crotchety old ladies in mink. Apparently they didn't like the feel of the air either, but they ate anyway.

Ashgrove moistened some food for the little kittens, who lay down on their portions and voiced murderous growls at anything they seemed to consider a threat. She looked out the back door; then she wandered up and looked out the front door. The wind still rose. The tulip trees and hickories stood to the storm, but the maples flung their heads around; zinc-pale sky and silver-pale underleaves glimmered between the branches. Everything that was still green seemed to have got even greener, fuller, and closer to the house; what she could see of the sky had an uneasy sulfurous tinge. She went and sat down on the back steps. The red flowers of the garden pulsated against the greens. Far off to the west it thundered heavily. A cool acid breath drifted from wet woods somewhere; maybe over the next ridge.

"It's going to come down a gullywomper," she said.

"The front's coming through," Martin's voice corrected.

She even thought she could see the storm: a slaty thickening off in the southern sky.

"They say that pigs can see the wind," she said. "Well, I wouldn't want to see it any better than this."

A kitten galloped up to the back door. Ashgrove reached behind her and grabbed it. It looked at her reproachfully, though it had learned not to say "Pt!" It was a little alien creature. Its tiny heart was driving wildly under its little striped ribs. She turned it loose. It skittered around and then began climbing up the screen.

The cat called Tom Scarborough stalked out of the hedge with a fell look on his broad face and a chipmunk squeaking in his jaws. Ashgrove shrieked, "Quit that!" Tom lumbered out of sight again. Ashgrove pressed her hand to her head.

The sound of an automobile engine came up the drive. There was a noise of backing and cutting around, as though the driver were turning the car's front wheels to the road in order to make a quick getaway.

It better be the séance people, she thought grimly. Nobody better mess with my chandeliers.

Howard and Emily Yeargin, walking rather close together, and carrying, among other things, a flashlight, entered the kitchen through the breezeway door.

"It was unlocked," Emily said. "Again."

"I'm going to have the cops out here for sure," Howard said. "This is too much."

Ashgrove came in through the back door, holding it open ostentatiously. The kitten stampeded in behind her. She let the door slam to.

"There she is," Emily said.

"Miss America," Ashgrove mimicked wildly. Then she thought, I'm getting hysterical.

"There's no one there, except the cat. I don't know what I was thinking of to bring you out here, Emily."

"Ashgrove, will you speak to my husband and tell him what you want? . . . My, your kitten has grown."

"Hasn't he? By leaps and bounds. . . . I really just want to be left alone. That's really all I want."

Emily looked uncertainly from Howard to Ashgrove and began to open a box that she had brought with her.

"Oh, good, Scrabble," Ashgrove said. "I used to be pretty good at Scrabble, and I'm getting tired of two-handed I Doubt It."

From several layers of paper bag Emily removed a wineglass, which she upturned on the round kitchen table. Then she began arranging Scrabble tiles in a semicircle, peering at each one to make sure that she had the complete alphabet. Howard stood trying to look detached.

"Why didn't you just bring a Ouija board?" Ashgrove asked sarcastically.

"The letters are what's important," Emily replied, "not what sort of board it is."

"Oh," Ashgrove said. She experimentally pushed the wineglass from one letter to another, spelling GO AWAY RIGHT NOW.

"Wait." Emily put one hand next to Ashgrove's on the bottom of the glass, but drew back immediately.

Howard said, "This is the damnedest thing. Make it spell some more."

Ashgrove spelled, I AM NOT NOW NOR HAVE I EVER BEEN AN IT.

"Where's my notebook?" Emily said. "I want to write this down."

"I'm going to light the lantern," Howard declared.

YOU BETTER NOT, Ashgrove spelled, but he was not watching.

No one had heard the second car arrive. Into the kitchen came two more people: Miss Alice Kinsolving, sensibly shod and voluminously scarved, and Mr. Gilchrist, who looked ruefully at the arrangement of letters and wineglass. Howard seemed pulled between embarrassment and relief. Emily seemed pleased. Ashgrove was not exactly sorry to see them come. She might have known: where there was trouble, there would be Mr. Gilchrist, and where there was anything interesting, there would be Miss Alice.

I suppose I must qualify as both.

"Good evening, Ashgrove," Miss Alice said.

"Miss Alice, really," Mr. Gilchrist said.

"Charles, the child is right there; if you don't see her, that's your problem. Who else doesn't see her? Mr. Yeargin? Well, what does that tell us about you gentlemen?"

Nobody answered. Ashgrove said, "I am not a child," and repeated this remark with the wineglass. "I'm starting to feel like one of those foreign movies with subtitles," she added.

"I'm starting to feel like Orestes and the Eumenides," Miss Alice said. "Only where has my friend Martin got to?"

Ashgrove wished that she knew herself.

"Mr. Gilchrist, I want you to advise this thing to go away," Howard said.

I AM NOT A THING EITHER, she spelled.

"No, I don't believe you are," the minister agreed. "Who are you then? Tell me."

She spelled her name.

174

"Are you here with us, Ashgrove?"

YES IVE ALWAYS BEEN RIGHT HERE

"Don't you want to be anywhere else?"

NO SIR WHERE ELSE WOULD I BE

"In my father's house are many mansions," the minister said.

THIS IS MY MANSION AND I DONT WANT TO LEAVE

"Charles, I think the girl might have a point."

"I have to offer her the choice."

"You mean brainwash her."

NO WAY

"Emily, are you getting all this?"

"Yes, but I can hardly see to write; I wish you'd light the lantern."

Howard struck a match to a large gasoline camping lantern and its white radiance filled the room with sharp, unfamiliar shadows. Before he could get the flame adjusted properly, Ashgrove quickly and firmly took it out of his hand and removed it to the breezeway, where she dropped it into the standby tub of water. It went out with a horrendous sizzle, and the chimney broke. Howard said, "Great God."

SORRY BUT THOSE THINGS WAY TOO DANGEROUS TERRIFY ME, Ashgrove spelled. She then lit one of her candles. THATS BETTER.

"Well, I guess that told you," Miss Alice said.

"An excellent thing is water," the preacher said.

"Charles, really."

"They are not dangerous; they're the safest kind you can get," Howard said angrily. Then he seemed surprised or sorry that he had responded. "Emily, you don't need to write all this."

"I think I ought to."

"Mr. Gilchrist, have you thought about getting in touch

with Francie Lee? She has this box number in New Orleans."

"Yes, but I don't think it would help her any."

"Help her? How about helping us?"

"Help who, do you mean?" Emily asked.

MAY I FIX EVERYONE SOME TEA Ashgrove felt herself mistress of the situation now. "I forgot," she added, "I only have two cups. Francie Lee got away with most of our dishes, and Sheridan, of course, did for the others."

"Sheridan indeed!" Miss Alice said. But no one had time to give her an odd look, for someone else was arriving at the back screen door. Ashgrove opened it and welcomed Jake. She was surprised to see that he had with him a youngish woman, redheaded and rawboned, whom he introduced to all as Ginny Reynolds.

Perhaps Ashgrove's judgment of people was as abnormally sharp as her night vision. Perhaps she would have guessed anyway; she had seen people before who held themselves carefully and looked at the same time both robustly healthy and about to faint. Anyway, she took one look and realized that Ginny Reynolds was pregnant.

There was conversation, awkward, as might be expected. It was really Mrs. Yeargin's séance, to which she had obviously invited neither Jake nor the woman named Ginny. Ashgrove had not invited anyone. She wished they would all leave, even Jake. She told them so, but they paid very little attention. Ginny Reynolds was looking quite ill; Jake brought her a drink of water, saying, "You should do this, Ashgrove."

She thought not. Then she was sorry. After all, it was almost a party, in spite of there not being enough cups to go around. At least she had enough chairs for all the women to sit. These were sweet people. Most of them had come here trying in their way to help her, despite fear of ridicule and whatever else might happen. Miss Alice was probably not afraid, though; she looked as though very little could faze her. Mr. Gilchrist she had always liked—skinny, silver-haired Mr. Gilchrist, who looked like a boy till he turned around and took off his hat—though she felt an intelligent man like him was wasted as a clergyman. Mrs. Yeargin had rouged and backcombed and tried to make herself look nice; she had come to help her husband, and Mr. Yeargin had come to look after his wife, as well as his investment.

So much was left that could threaten these people. She felt a painful urge to protect them.

Still, the situation had its funny side. The conflict in Howard Yeargin was rampantly apparent. Here he was with two women who claimed to see a ghost and another man who could not. The other man had the authority of the clergy. Thus the ghost must be some feminine hallucination. Then came two unexpected visitors: a bearded man who could see the ghost, unless he was bluffing, and an exhausted-looking woman who was gazing around the room with bewilderment and had hardly said a word.

Ashgrove, still in an access of hospitality, began to spell, I WOULD OFFER YOU ALL SOME TEA BUT—Then came the familiar racket of the old steam engine; familiar to her, but to almost no one else. "The fort is relieved," she said, to cover her own relief.

Everyone else showed varying degrees of alarm and stupefaction. Martin entered through the back door, looking exactly the same as ever, as though he had never left. But she hardly had time to be glad or sorry to see him, for someone else came in behind him. Or something else.

She summoned up all her nerve and volume and cried in rage and dismay, "Get that thing out of my kitchen!"

# 9

GINNY REYNOLDS had never yet spoken to Redfern.

Well, you blew it that time, Ginny.

Well, maybe not. Maybe he's the one who blew it.

During these days of September, she seemed to herself to live in suspension, outside time; it always amazed her to note that, on the calendar, time was passing. Her waist was thickening, just a little; her breasts were getting even heavier. Ginny was a big girl and built to carry weight. She never looked right in her clothes; in fact, she had often thought that she looked better without them. This was her own idea; neither Redfern nor anyone else had suggested it to her.

Time was indeed passing; the days were shortening, the

light was changing. It lay more and more horizontally on the fields and woods, turning the sycamores and corn-fields more yellowish than ever and bringing a slaty blue back to the sky in the late afternoons. Ginny had taken a great liking to Mason County and the whole Piedmont, partly because of having originally come from the flat piny Tidewater, which held few surprises of contour or color. She drove the back roads while she might. When she got big enough to be conspicuous, she would probably change from field work to office work.

I already *am* big enough to be conspicuous. I always was.

Sometimes, on one of the back roads to Richmond, she would drive past a certain house, which she always noticed because she had to slow down there for the curve. Southbound, there was a sharp bend to the right, and then to the left again as the road corrected its course, and beyond the bend, beyond the big sycamore, almost invisible behind overgrown hedges, could just be seen the tall gables of a house, and its thick chimneys and wide-set windows. She had never stopped there. There was no one living there, nothing to stop for, and every reason not to stop. At best, while trying to get to some client's house, she might put her wheel in the ditch in the line of duty. Virginia's roads were well and truly ditched. She did not need to get stranded while off on some wild goose chase. Some wild house chase.

Still, it had been so dry lately. The roads and ditches were as passable as they would ever be. Homeward bound late one muggy Friday afternoon, having dealt with her last client for the day, Ginny looked into the rear-view mirror of her Volkswagen, saw no one pressing behind her, and threw a left into Ashgrove's driveway, which at that time she did not know belonged to Ashgrove. She thought of it as Frazier's place, since that was the name on the rusty, tilting mailbox.

She cut her engine and got out, standing with one hand on the window frame of the car.

Nothing happened. Nothing at all. All was quiet under the thick, pale sky. The birds were not even saying much, though lately the mockingbirds had begun trying to sing again, with a cidery sweetness. The quietness there could consume you, make you feel that you didn't exist. She took a step closer to the house, and the dry grass lisped underfoot. It was a tall, big old house, not any style at all. It had grayish-green shutters, a grayish-green attic roof and porch roof; it was half smothered in yellowish-green wisteria and starred with reddening Virginia creeper. A FOR SALE OR RENT sign lay on its back, flung down in the pale dry grass.

Her nerves prickled. Her bladder prickled. She experienced a pressing urge to relieve it, but thought that she had best not. God knows who might suddenly show up on the scene. She drove on back toward town and turned left at the next crossroad in search of a filling station, this being a shortcut to the federal highway. The station she found did not even accept her credit card. She bought a dollar's worth of regular and dashed for the john. The man wiped her windshield anyway.

For someone whose job was with people, Ginny was rather solitary. Most of her colleagues at work were married women whose time outside office hours was taken up with their own families and did not include entertaining a casual single. Ginny had not minded; most of her time off had been concerned with Redfern anyway, in one way or another. The truth was that dealing with people as she did—unfortunate people—poor, sick, disturbed, hostile, or fawning—tended to disincline her for much sociability. Still, she had pride in her job. If she didn't do it, who would? Someone who might do it worse.

That wasn't pride in her job. It was pride in herself.

Egoism was a fact of life. You did what you could, but there it still was, and maybe nothing would get done without it.

She was tired now at day's end. She wanted to be quiet. Take a bath. Read a magazine. Get some nice music on the radio. Go to sleep early. She was letting herself into her kitchen—that which had once been the butler's pantry—when she realized that someone was in there waiting for her.

It was a little person. Ginny had six inches on her, and fifty pounds. It was Mrs. Franklin, the landlady.

Help.

"What is it, Mrs. Franklin? Is something wrong?"

"I came here after I gave Franklin his supper. I didn't want him to know I came. I don't want him to know about you."

Ginny slumped in the doorway and unobtrusively eased off her shoes.

"Well, I'm hardly a secret."

"Huzzy. Slut. I've watched you. I know your secret."

Ginny set her face in a mild, impassive stare. She must show no uncertainty or weakness here; the fertilizer had hit the fan sooner than she had expected.

"If I wasn't a good Christian woman, you'd find your stuff thrown out on the street."

"I suppose we all ought to be thankful that you're a good Christian woman."

The old woman's color was not good. Her lips were bluish and her complexion muddy. She said in a voice tight with hatred and pain, "Revolutionary! Communist agitator."

"Oh, come on. I'd never have got my job, if that were so."

181

"Taking our money and spending it on blacks and white trash. Paying them to have babies. You're no better than them anyway."

What was the answer?

No, and neither are you; none of us are, when it comes right down to it; smarter, maybe, and more organized, but not better.

If your church were a good Christian church, it would help those people who needed help, and the government wouldn't have to do it.

There wasn't any answer. Ugly words cloaked things that those who spoke them could never express: fear of change, frustration from stretching a small income over constantly rising expenses, weariness of carrying around a sick and aging body, jealousy of someone who was still young and fairly untroubled. The desire to make trouble, to give frustration.

There was nothing she could say. Mrs. Franklin would accept nothing from her now. She adopted her best counselor's voice: "What I hear you saying is you want me to move out, right?"

"I'll give you a week. If you're not out of here by then, I'm putting you out."

"I doubt it will come to that."

"You're not getting your rent back either."

"I don't want it."

Mrs. Franklin stumbled out, moving unsteadily.

I should have begged for my rent. I knew she wanted me to. That would have made her a little happier.

Oh, damnation.

Ginny turned and threw up, inaudibly, she hoped, into the kitchen sink.

Then she took a bath and changed into comfortable clothes.

What else could she do?

She spread that day's *Aegis* out on the kitchen table to read while she drank her broth, and sighed. She had seen both movies playing in town, and the library was closed on Friday nights. Of course, there was always the high-school football game, but she thought not, on the whole. She turned to the real-estate page.

Masonborough was not well supplied with apartments. Usually if you lived there, you had a house. Many of the existing apartments were of the same sort as Mrs. Franklin's, sharing a portion of an old house with its landlady. Mrs. Franklin would probably be promptly on the horn to the rest of the sisterhood, advising them with slavering lips not to rent to scarlet Ginny Reynolds and family.

She went to the phone and dialed as far as 555 of long-distance information. Then she dropped the receiver and turned back to the newspaper.

Howard Yeargin's realty company was one of the big ones. It seemed to have a large selection of listings. Where had she heard that name before? In connection with something interesting or odd? It was about all she could do to keep her clients straight, much less everyone else. Oh. The name on the sign, out by the old house that afternoon, had been Howard Yeargin.

It had said it was for rent, as well as for sale.

I could never afford it.

Sometimes one could find country property going real cheaply. The house looked as though it'd been empty awhile.

Maybe I could get in to see it anyhow. Threaten Mrs. Franklin and maybe she'll change her mind.

She went back to the phone. Howard's office was closed, but she reached him at his home number. "This is

Eugenia Reynolds. I was interested in an old house that you are offering." She described the location as best she could. "And the mailbox said Frazier."

"Well, Mrs. Reynolds, if you could leave your number, I could call you back on that. The fact is, I'm expecting some developments that will change things. I mean, for the better."

"Oh," Ginny said, at a loss. What could he mean, for the better? Raise the price? She docilely gave him her number.

"So I'll call you back on that," Howard Yeargin repeated, sounding distracted. "And will you excuse me now? I have something fairly urgent to attend to."

"Howard!" called a female voice in the background.

They hung up.

He had called her Mrs. Reynolds. Maybe she sounded married. Probably he thought anyone looking for a house would surely be married. Everyone tonight seemed to be operating on some other wavelength. A noticeably weird wavelength. Why not? The weather was weird. It had grown thundery enough to turn milk, steamy and damp-smelling. Her apartment was stuffy and caught none of the breeze that pushed from the south and west.

She collected a thermos of hot broth and a poncho, on the off chance that it might turn cooler. She had decided to drive out to the old house, lock herself in the car, listen to the radio, and just vegetate, safe behind the hedge, away from this place full of cooking smells and angry old voices.

She got into her Volkswagen again and drove down the federal highway with her foot in the gas tank. Then she turned left onto the road over which she had come that afternoon. It was still too hot for broth. Here was that gas station. She needed a soda pop, if it was still open.

It was definitely still open. Someone was there, anyway. It was a kind of country-store concern, offering work clothes, chewing tobacco, lamp oil, "the whole schmier," as Redfern would say. Light poured out of the upstairs window, as well as music: Jimmy Reed, mournful and galvanic.

Ginny felt she knew all she wanted or needed to know about good old boys, but still she wondered what kind of good old boys could possibly be in there.

A man came out past the gas pumps to her car. "Yes, ma'am," he said. It was probably the same man of that afternoon—heavy-set and heavily bearded. She had not exactly been too embarrassed to look at him, but she still hadn't taken much notice. Perhaps he hadn't noticed her either; anyway, then she had been wearing a dress.

"I just came to get a soda pop," she said. "I'm sorry I drove over your ringer." She added, "Maybe you could tell me about this Frazier house over here."

Jake Galey said, "Such as what?" He was uncertain what else to add.

The woman got out. She was probably in her late twenties, sturdily built, and much of a height with himself, dressed in tight Levi's and a thin loose blouse with embroidered trim. Her reddish hair was long and pulled back from her face. She leaned against her car door, balancing her keys in her hand.

She said, "I honestly don't understand why everyone is so cagey. I was just talking to Howard Yeargin—you know who I mean? The realtor. He mumbled something and said he'd call back. I'd have thought he'd be interested in showing houses, but I'm beginning to feel like Jane Eyre. Does he keep a mad wife someplace?"

A person less like Jane Eyre than this girl would be hard

to imagine. Jake toyed with the notion that she was built like a Canadian outhouse. But he only said, "Well . . . Howard's wife . . . I don't know. She's not mad enough to be locked up. I don't suppose I owe Howard any favors. No. Not to Howard. Are you telling me you're different from everybody else? Do you really not know already all there is to know about the Frazier place?"

"What is there to know?"

Maybe nothing for sure. Just plenty of gossip."

"I guess I haven't heard it. Maybe I just haven't talked to the right people. My profession isn't always smiled upon," she said, grinning slightly. "I'm a social worker."

"You don't look like one."

"What am I supposed to look like? Anyway, it's Friday night. T.G.I.F. I left my uniform at home. What was the gossip? I'm really not a revolutionary agitator, in spite of what some people may think."

"Well, you don't look like one of those either."

"Thanks." She fell silent, obviously not liking to question him any more.

"About the gossip," Jake said. "You haven't heard that the Frazier house is haunted?"

"Supposed to be haunted?"

"Is haunted."

"By what? Or who?"

"You said you wanted a soda. Are you still thirsty? Come on in the store and I'll give you one. I don't know everyone around here either, and I don't believe I know you. I'm Jake Galey."

She smiled again, as though to herself, and told him she was Ginny Reynolds.

Inside, he pulled out two drinks from the cooler, where the bottles stood up to their shoulders in ice water. The electric bulb showed that Ginny's face and bare arms were freckled and that she had eyes the color of strong tea. The music had changed; it was Chuck Berry now.

He said distinctly, "Now, about the ghosts."

"Ghosts? Two? More?"

"Occupancy by more than two ghosts is both illegal and unlawful. No, seriously, you're right; there are two."

"Have you seen them then? What are they like?"

"They're just like you and me, only different."

"That helps a lot."

"It seems that either you can see them or you can't. If you can, you'll know what I mean. If you can't, I guess you won't know."

"Can you talk to them?"

"Sometimes. Depending. What do you want to go there for?"

"Well, I wanted to see the house. I might not have enough money, but I was interested in it. I like old houses. I'm living in one now, but it's not quite what I hoped for. I was thinking about moving. But of course I hadn't considered moving to a haunted house."

"I was cagey with you at first because I thought you were just another tourist. Howard Yeargin has been half distracted by rubberneckers, or so I hear. For that matter, so have Ashgrove and Martin."

"You mean the ghosts? Those are their names?"

"That's right."

"I could coexist with ghosts, I suppose. I just want some time to myself. I'll leave them alone if they'll leave me alone."

"They mostly use the kitchen, I think."

"They're welcome to it. What do they *do*? Scream? Materialize? Pinch people? Plait their hair? Go bump in the night?"

"Mainly they just argue. He looks at her, and she looks

187

at him, and they argue. When they say anything at all. She's also about a foot shorter than he is."

"Well, if I see any people who answer that description, I'll know who they are."

"You really want to take a look out there?"

"Yes, I did, but it's getting so dark now."

"Well, if you still want to go, I'll take you. I was going anyway. I'm getting this all screwed up, but probably the reason why Howard Yeargin wouldn't talk to you was that he and his wife are coming out here to hold a séance. With the idea of getting the ghosts to clear out of the house."

"Do you think that will work?"

"No. Neither do they."

"Howard and his wife?"

"Martin and Ashgrove."

"Then what do you think will happen?"

"God only knows, but it promises to be interesting. Come on. We can go in my car. . . . Looks like we're finally going to have some rain. Listen to that thunder."

The music stopped by itself. Jake locked his store, put up his CLOSED sign, and brought with him a large flashlight. He put Ginny into his car and got in himself. The engine was cold and hard to start. Perhaps something was wrong with the choke. They jolted off, the speedometer cable flapping like a loose halyard in a high wind. Ginny thought this car was in even worse shape than her own.

"I'm going to go around the back way," Jake said.

Ginny wondered what the alleged back way might be and how long it would take. Instead of going down the county road, they turned right on an old field road that paralleled the main-line railroad. It had gotten dark earlier than it should. Or the days were shorter than ever, this close to the first day of fall. The sky was black with thunderheads, and the wind shoved and thrust uneasily. Perhaps she should have taken her car and gone on somewhere else, even though Jake Galey had a wholesome, stone-ground look, and she was old enough and big enough to take care of herself.

She said, "What am I doing? I don't have any business coming to this."

"It's all right. Let me put it this way, if you don't mind. You won't exactly be the center of attraction, if the ghosts show. And if they *don't* show, and you're at all interested in the house, Howard Yeargin will be interested in you. So it's okay."

"Will I really know it, if they show?"

"Oh, you'll know all right. They aren't exactly like everyone else."

"I thought you said they were."

"Well, they are and they aren't," Jake said.

Ginny could think of no reply to this. She gave up asking questions, even though there was more that she wanted to know. How had the ghosts happened to come there? How long had they been there? What kind of name was Ashgrove? And where did this man get off, as the authority on it all? But she felt silly voicing these questions even to herself, even supposing that she would get any answers.

"All right. This is the roughest part of the trip, but we'll be there in a minute." He pushed the car into an even lower gear and aimed it at the grade that took the field road to the left over the railroad tracks.

Ginny said, "Jake. Do you hear something?"

"My God." He threw on his brakes, and the engine died—not on the track itself, but on the slope just below it.

They were never able to agree afterward on what

189

actually happened, if anything did. The sound of thunder, groaning and grumbling far away, came closer and merged with another sound: a steam locomotive at full throttle, throwing on all its brakes, its whistle yelling like the damned, tortured metal screaming. And there were other screams too. Jake said later that he saw the engine, and the tail end of the halted train ahead of it: the flares, the blinding headlight, the sparks flying out of the stack and thrown from the five-foot drivers. "If she hadn't turned over so fast I'd've seen how many wheels she had and what kind she was." But she turned on her side—the boiler scattering fiery ruin, the flying pistons digging the trackbed—and then she was gone. They could only see the glint of the rails, empty and undisturbed under a sky swollen with clouds and the smothered twilight of moonrise. The smell of the wreck still hung on the air a few seconds—heavy bituminous smoke, reeking with sulfur, metal hotter than it was ever meant to be, and something much worse even than that—then it, too, was gone.

"Lightning plays odd tricks sometimes," Jake said. "Something got struck somewhere."

"Ahhhh," Ginny groaned. She lay back in her seat. He switched on the dome light, but she shut her eyes against it, then flung the door open and quietly vomited. She had eaten very little, so she was soon done. The drink came up and left her more dehydrated than ever.

"All right, it wasn't lightning," Jake said. He offered her his handkerchief.

"Thanks," she managed to say. "I'm sorry."

"Why? Because you were scared enough to vomit? At least you saw it too."

"Ah, God."

"Would you like to go back and get your car? I bet you don't feel like driving."

"I don't know. I'd like some water."

"We're almost to Ashgrove's place now. She has a good well. I guess it's safe to go on," Jake said. He cautiously restarted his car and ground it up the grade. Nothing else happened. Ginny wiped her lips and forehead and wrapped the handkerchief around her clammy hands.

They left the car near the barn and walked slowly, flashlit, from there to the house. Ginny breathed shallowly and wished that she had a little water.

A light could be seen flickering from the back kitchen windows. Probably candlelight, Jake said. They reached the back door and Jake rapped at the screen. It opened, and an earnest, anxious voice said, "Oh, Jake, I'm so glad you've got here. You wouldn't believe all that's been going on. I don't know where Martin is, but I just extinguished their lantern in the water tub. They weren't best pleased."

"Well, for God's sake, Ashgrove, I can sure see why not."

"Better their lantern than *my house*," insisted the voice, which belonged to a child, or a young woman no bigger than a large twelve-year-old. The big, dim old kitchen was lit by one candle, and even in its light she was pale, and obviously driven completely by nerves.

Standing about the round kitchen table were four other people, who were introduced as Mr. and Mrs. Yeargin, Miss Kinsolving, the librarian, and Mr. Gilchrist, the minister. Upon the table sat an odd assembly of lettered tiles and a wineglass.

"I'm Ashgrove Frazier," the girl said.

Ginny's eyes widened, and she wet her lips.

"I need to get this lady some water," Jake said. "We had a rough trip over here. Nearly saw a bad wreck."

Ginny sat down suddenly in the basket chair. Jake got a

cup off the drainboard and started out the door to the breezeway. He added, addressing everyone in the room, "Any luck?"

"Depends on what you call luck," Howard said.

"She's definitely here," Emily said.

"There's some sort of presence," Mr. Gilchrist said.

"Oh!" Miss Kinsolving said. "There's nothing wrong with that child that a good spanking wouldn't fix right up. And don't you glare at me, Ashgrove."

"I'm right with you, Miss Kinsolving," Jake said, from outside.

"People!" Emily cried. "Please don't antagonize her! We want to be able to help her, and you're just making her mad."

"I just want all of you to go away," Ashgrove Frazier said, looking distraught in the extreme. Ginny laid her head back in the chair. A calico cat dashed in and leaped like a bomb into her unprepared lap. After the shock had worn off, she cradled it till it ran off again. At least one other cat peered with round eyes from the top of some cupboard, and several kittens stormed around underfoot.

Ashgrove went on, "What is it going to take? Am I going to have to come on like a poltergeist and break things and throw ashes around? That's so uncouth. I really hate it. It's the lowest of the low."

Jake returned with the cup of water. Ginny took a little gratefully. "Anybody else want any? You should be doing this, Ashgrove."

The girl just looked at him skeptically. Then she began to move the wineglass on the table, pushing it back and forth as though to spell out something, but Ginny never found out what it was, for a noise came on their ears and everyone leaped for the back door—everyone except Ginny, who could not make herself get up.

Jake said, "Ginny, I believe you'll find it's all right this time."

What she heard now was not the full-throated roar of a big locomotive, but an almost toylike puffing. It grew louder as it came closer, throbbing and banging. It was coming up toward the back of the house from the barnyard—or from the railroad track? Ginny thought wildly.

"What the hell *is* that?" Howard said.

"I'll tell you in . . . just a minute," Mr. Gilchrist said.

"Oh, *no*," Emily said.

Miss Kinsolving began to laugh.

"I believe it's the armor," Jake said. He sounded amused too.

"It's the U.S. Cavalry," Ashgrove said. "The fort is relieved."

*Eeeek*, said a piercing whistle.

Ginny had reached the back door by this time. They were all crowded together there, shoulder to shoulder. They all saw it, spotlit by somebody's flashlight. It was really there, and not about to vanish. Ginny had never before laid eyes on such a thing; her times in Washington had not taken her to the more arcane reaches of the Smithsonian. "It's Mr. Frazier's tractor," someone said. But it was like no tractor that she had ever seen; more like some tiny pufferbilly locomotive in an old-fashioned color engraving.

The tractor—engine—whatever it was—veered across the grass of the backyard and around the drive to the front of the house. It could then be heard grinding to a clattering halt.

Ginny never saw who was manning its big iron steering wheel.

"That isn't Martin!" Ashgrove cried. "Where is he?"

"Nowhere—I'm right here," a new voice said. The screen door opened and closed quickly, and someone pushed past them, gesturing as if to wipe dark hair off his forehead. Under what was left of his sunburn he looked even more weary and baffled than Ginny felt. He and the girl were the youngest people there, the one scarcely coming up to the other one's shoulder. They glared at each other with hostile concern, as though they had the kitchen to themselves.

"Then tell me who that was," Ashgrove said to him.

"You had well ask. I'll be damned if I know. He wouldn't take any mess, though. Just helped himself to my engine."

"Engine, hell," said still another voice, dry and grating. "Call that an engine?" The door swung open again, as though flapped by the rising wind, and they all fell back before what came in this time: a ball of soft reddish light a couple of feet from the floor, about the level of a lantern carried in a man's hand.

I can't pass out now, Ginny told herself.

If this were in my field, what a paper it would be.


"Get that *lantern* out of my *kitchen*," Ashgrove shrieked. She was thoroughly terrified and about to lose her temper at the same time.

"Young lady," said the bearer of the lantern, swiveling around slowly, "curb that clattering tongue."

"I'd advise that you do what he says, Ashgrove," Martin said. He moved over beside her, and she took hold of his elbow. He was as cold as the Celtic hell, but familiar; he also seemed fairly unflappable.

The visitant was certainly not familiar. He looked drastically ill treated, as though he had been in a fight. Then she realized that he had been in worse than a fight. He had been in a train wreck.

194

She never afterward remembered his face at all. He was medium tall, slightly built, and of indeterminate age. His hair might have been blond or gray. He wore the decent navy suit and flat silver-badged cap of the old-time trainman, and still carried the flagman's lantern. But his clothes were torn and filthy, smeared with dark and greasy stains, and between his head and shoulders gaped a terrible dark place that was either a shadow or a wound.

He stared inimically at everyone in the room—those alive and those not. They stood in a stunned, ragged semicircle. No one thought to ask him to spell with the letters. Howard Yeargin stood with his hand on Emily's shoulder, and Mr. Gilchrist raised his head, listening hard to every word.

"I'm the oldest person here," Alice Kinsolving said, "and I can't see you very well, but I know who you are."

"Then say my name. Say it."

"You're Joe McIntosh. People looked for you for a long time, then they didn't go out there any more. They forgot you."

"I just found my head after ninety years. No thanks to anyone here."

"That's why Mr. Mac was so odd to me," Emily told Howard. "It was his uncle." She sounded pleased to have a handle on something.

"Why was it our fault?" Alice asked Joe. "Why did it take ninety years?"

"It has to be three things, before I can come back—a thunderstorm and full moon, because that's the way it was the night I was killed—and people have to be watching."

"Like Emily Dickinson's poems."

"Oh, hush, Martin."

"No one came. People used to come. On thundery nights, people would sit there by the tracks and court, and wait to see me going up and down with my lantern, looking for my head. Finally tonight, people came, and I found it."

Ginny Reynolds found her voice. "We were *not* courting. And no one but a complete freak would sit around waiting for something like that . . . horror show. I even threw up. Call that courting?" she added bitterly. "We just met, actually."

Jake said equably, "Well, to each his own."

"Horror show," Joe said, with contempt. "It was no show. I was in it. We didn't have any block signals or any radio like they have now. Oh, I know what they have now. I ought to know. But we ran trains by the seat of our pants in those days. My train was stopped on the side track. We were pulling a string of varnish, excursion coming back from Washington. The bridge was out up ahead. It had been terrible rainy weather. Didn't clear the main line all the way, so I went back to put down some flares. But the hotshot freight plowed right into me and my train too."

"You were brave," Miss Alice said.

"I didn't save the train. It was an awful wreck . . . Oh, no. I won't tell."

"We know," Ginny said.

"You better know," Joe said.

Martin said, "I want to know how you found your head if you didn't have it in the first place. How could you see where it was?"

"I don't rightly remember. . . . It was under a clump of sumac bushes. . . . I think *it* saw *me*."

"So what are you going to do now?" Martin pressed.

"*Do?* I don't know. Everything's different now. They're building everything up. And some places are deserted. And the steam engines are all gone. When did they take them away? After that last big war? I always notice wars. People would always do a lot of courting during wars. I found my head, and I wondered which way to go. I remembered this house. This was Frazier's place. It had just been built then. There wasn't as much of it. They've added on. Is it still Frazier's place?"

"Yes," Ashgrove said. "I'm the Frazier." She was recovering her poise, pretending to have a dirk in her stocking and be the head of the table.

"You don't look much like a Frazier. They were tall, handsome people."

"I do so. My grandfather wouldn't like to hear you say that."

"Is your grandfather still alive, girl?"

"No. I'm not either. Would you like to stay here and haunt with me? The house is plenty big."

"Oh, God," Martin said. "This is where I came in."

"I'm *leaving*," Joe said. "I came up from the railroad and found this young fellow working with a rig I never expected to see."

"I was shot out of the saddle," Martin said. "He told me, 'You're in a heap of trouble,' and rode off on it."

"They took the steam engine away. There's only that little one left. How could they do that? They breathe and sigh in their sleep like a woman. You have to feed 'em and water 'em and coax 'em like a baby. They scream like a woman too. I'm dead, but the steam is always warm, and always breathing."

Joe wheeled suddenly and flung himself out the back door, taking the light of his red lantern with him. The tractor coughed into life again and bore off down the land, then turned south, heading away from town, making better speed than Martin had ever been able to get from it, and the whistle shrieking like all lost America.

"Well," Ashgrove said. She was the only one readily able to speak. "That's exactly the way men are. Get wheels under 'em and zap, they're gone. Happens every single time."

They all seemed to be standing outside without knowing how they had got there. And it had begun to rain, after threatening for so long. First big drops came down inches apart, hardly comprehensible or credible. Then there began, as Ashgrove had foretold, a gullywomper. Those who were worried about getting wet made for the house.

But Martin raised his face to the rain. "The monsoons have set in," he said.

"We really needed this," Ashgrove said. "It will sure help the farmers."

"I can do without it."

"I know you can. You can do without everything. There isn't anything you can't do without."

"I sure didn't know it would prickle like this."

"Do come back to the house. I have to find out what else is going to happen."

"Nothing would surprise me," he said. "All right; I'll come. I wanted to see you anyway."

"Did you ever imagine anyone like that would appear on the scene?"

"I think it's fairly obvious: no."

They slipped in quietly, but no one in the kitchen was looking in their direction; they were all looking at one another, each seemingly wondering who would speak first.

"All right, what did everyone see?" Howard Yeargin finally said.

"Nothing, really," the minister said. "I knew they were there, but I couldn't reach them."

"I saw them," Ginny said. "Two of them."

Emily looked at her husband and at the other visitors. "So did I—yes, I saw two of them."

"And the lantern," Ginny added with an effort.

"And the lantern."

"And I heard what he said."

"Same here," Jake said.

"Yes. We all did."

They all leaned together in a little knot of tired people.

"There were three of them," Miss Kinsolving said. "The boy and the girl and Joe McIntosh. I wonder what will become of Joe, by the way. I hope I find out."

No one in that age of Mason County ever learned what became of Joe. But the engine was discovered the next day lying in the ditch by the back road to Richmond. Perhaps Martin had not left enough water in it. Perhaps Joe did something ill advised to the safety valve or the draft. It had overheated and cracked in two like an old teakettle, though with considerably more force. It was hauled away by an antique dealer, who was glad to get it, and it ended its days as an advertisement, sitting beside U.S. 29 over in Culpeper County.

From this time also dated the slow upturn in the fortunes of Emily, who began to enjoy much more esteem and favor than she had ever had before. Her husband had finally decided that she brought him luck, of a sort that he could not afford to do without.

Ginny Reynolds, trying to get the situation back on an everyday level, said, "Mr. Yeargin, what I wanted to ask you—"

"Oh. Are you the Mrs. Reynolds who called me this evening?"

"Well, yes. And did I understand this house was for rent? I'm interested in privacy, and I expect I'll get it here."

"I doubt anyone will come out here at all any more," Emily said. "You'll have an awful time getting domestic help."

"Emily."

"Oh, never mind."

"Well, it's late, but we could still talk business if you care to." Howard seemed glad of the prospect.

He offered to drive her to get her car. She accepted, told Jake thanks for the ride, and good-bye to the older people. Mr. Gilchrist invited her to church. She half promised to go.

Miss Kinsolving, with a sphinxlike grin, said, "Child, if they give you any trouble, I know everybody who is anybody." But that could have meant almost anything.

"It's been," Jake said. He got up to leave.

"Don't go, Jake," Ashgrove said. She unaccountably did not want the party to be over.

"You haven't got anything I want to drink, Ashgrove."

"I could fix everyone some tea now, since there are fewer of us."

"I would like some tea," Miss Alice said. "Charles, would you like some tea?"

"Yes, I believe I would," the minister said abstractedly. He was sitting in one of the straight chairs, very still, almost withdrawn into himself. Miss Alice took the other straight chair.

Ashgrove had to revive the fire and refill the kettle. It all took time. Jake and Martin stood on opposite sides of the back door, not saying a word. No one else spoke either, not even Ashgrove herself, except once to apologize for having no sugar. She sensed that everyone wanted badly to talk but that no one felt it was the right time. She made some strong spearmint tea, one of her more successful blends. Miss Alice and Mr. Gilchrist drank theirs attentively. Mr. Gilchrist bowed his head over his cup, and Ashgrove wondered if he was praying.

To her mind, he belonged in the church, speaking gently from the pulpit with those broad lowland vowels—"Oh, darely, darely has he loved!" He haunted the pulpit just as she haunted her house, just as Miss Alice would always haunt the library in a thousand ways, not least by her neat pen-lettering marching across the mended spines of books.

"Charles, why are you so quiet? Are you moping? Are you sorry that you couldn't see any ghosts?" Miss Alice mocked him blandly. Who but Miss Alice would have the nerve to speak to the preacher like that? Ashgrove thought. "Don't worry. After I'm gone I'll come back and haunt you. You'll get to see one ghost if it's the last thing I do."

"You and Houdini, Miss Alice," Mr. Gilchrist replied, startling everyone.

"Will you take me home now, Charles? It's late. Our kinfolk will worry." She swept up the end of her woolen stole, and Mr. Gilchrist squired her out the door. "Good night, Ashgrove. Good night, gentlemen. Martin, I already told you good-bye, so I won't prolong it."

"And then there were three," Ashgrove said. "Tell us about your friend, Jake. Is it Mrs. Reynolds or Miss Reynolds?"

"She didn't say. She just drove up and asked directions to your place. So I said I'd drive her over. She seemed serious, brighter than the others, and I figured she might as well know the worst. Do you know you practically have a sound-and-light show going on over there at Frazier's Crossing? I wonder how often in every ninety years that goes on."

"I knew it. I knew it. I always knew there was something peculiar about Frazier's Crossing. My grandfather never mentioned a thing to me about it. He was so

Presbyterian he would have thought it was of the devil. He never even knew about my deck of cards."

"You think that lady Reynolds is going to move into this house?" Martin asked. "I'd say from the looks of her she didn't have the cash, but you never know; she may be an eccentric millionaire, or kin to one."

"I'll tell you something else from the looks of her," Ashgrove said deliberately. "She's a little bit pregnant."

Jake and Martin both stared at her severely. She went on: "I wouldn't think you'd have to be very smart to figure that out."

Then they both spoke at once. "It's not a matter of being smart. It's a matter of couth."—"You'd just have to be smart enough not to say anything."

"Oh. Well . . ." She was cut. She had really lost face. The worst was that they were still looking at her without saying another word. "My grandfather always said I tended to go along with my mouth in high gear and my brain in neutral." This was as close to an apology as she would offer. "I'm really going to have to stay now and find out what will happen. I can't miss anything."

"Well, remember what I said, Ashgrove," Jake told her more gently.

"Oh, go away, Jake."

He turned toward the back door.

"No, don't."

"No, I have to."

"Well, Jake, I just want to leave you with one thought: They that sow in tears shall reap in melancholia."

Jake said, "There's a lot more truth and a lot less humor in that than you might think."

"Good-bye now, Jake," Martin said.

He and Ashgrove faced each other across the kitchen table. Rain hit the tin roof relentlessly.

# 10

"WELL, MARTIN, I must admit, you did good there. You were the only one who wasn't flabbergasted."

"I don't flabbergast easy, any more."

"You want to sit down and have a cup of coffee?"

"No, I don't think so."

"Well, then," Ashgrove said. What to do for him, or with him? " 'Fare thee well, and if forever, then forever fare thee well.' "

"So you're really not going to go away with me. Just business as usual. Back at the old stand."

"This is my chance! No one will ever come back here now! Joe *saved* me."

"From what?"

"Having to leave. Imagine that. He was here all along

and I didn't know it. And a grumly guest I'm sure was he. Worse than you. No telling who else is here. Or what else."

"*I* am here. But not for much longer."

" 'I'm leaving,' he said absently. 'I'm going to California,' he stated."

"Aren't you going to ask me what I did all day?"

"Well, what did you do all day?"

"I went into town—Masonborough."

"Ah. Storied Masonborough."

"One-storied Masonborough."

"The nerve."

"And I walked around. And nobody saw me, except Miss Alice. She said Hi. So I went in and talked to her on her lunch break."

"I bet you timed the whole deal for her lunch break."

"Well, what of it? I didn't bother anybody and they didn't bother me. After all, they didn't have anything I wanted, and I didn't have anything they wanted. I was glad I went. But I thought I'd come back one more time, and see how you were getting along. Last time I saw you, you were passed out on the ground."

"Well, you saw how I was doing. I had a party in progress."

"A real blast from the past."

"That is not funny, Martin. You think it is, but it isn't."

"When nothing is funny, then everything is. Right?"

"I wouldn't know."

"I'd've thought that you would."

"Well, I don't," she said.

"He was really something, wasn't he?"

"Yes. Something else."

"Do we have to stand here talking all the rest of the night?"

"Why not? I'm quite capable of it."

"Ashgrove, what did Jake mean? Remember what he said?"

"He said different things at different times. Some I remember and some I don't. And some I repressed."

"Ashgrove, there really isn't anyone else here, is there? You're the only one."

"And you."

"We're talking in circles. It's time for me to go now. Are you coming?"

"Aren't you afraid? You won't have any place to *be*."

"Maybe so, maybe not. If I have to stay in one place to exist, then I'd as soon not exist," Martin said. "If all I have is to look on, I'm for damn sure going to look on at a lot of places. Not just the courthouse square."

"*What?*"

"Something that happened a long time ago."

"Furthermore, you won't have anybody nice to talk to."

"There are people out there you can talk to. You meet them when you least expect it. Like Miss Alice."

"She's *old*."

"It's an occupational hazard. You get it from being alive. Now. I want my . . . oh."

She fetched his guitar out of the corner. "I brought it up from the barn when I moved back in." If not for me, you wouldn't have it at all, she thought. She also wondered how he planned to get it from place to place, but refrained from saying so. That was his problem.

"Thanks," he said, courteous as always, or almost always.

You won't have anybody to look after you, she thought, but she didn't say that either. He looked extremely migratory. She raised the fat dripping candle, realizing that she had never watched him as closely as she would have liked, never really learned the pattern of his face. He stood there, long and lanky, unshaven and faded, graceful as a cat, yet awkwardly poised as though for some crazy sideways spring. He was a trick of the light, a corollary to some little-known law of the universe, a shadow among shadows.

"You weren't like that mixed-up duck after all," she said.

"I never was. And you're not like that big collie dog, either; you just thought you were."

"What kind of animal am I like?"

"I don't want to play that game," he said.

Setting her mouth in mockery, she said, "He wouldn't go ahead, nor he wouldn't stand still, so he went up and down like an old sawmill."

He said, "That isn't you, Ashgrove. I've done all the arguing I'm going to do. Tell me good-bye."

"Sir, you and I must part, but there's not it. . . . That isn't me either. It's a quotation. I bet you don't know who said it. You'd laugh if you did."

"I could tell it was a quotation. You'd never call me sir if it weren't."

"Can't think of anything else," she said helplessly.

"That definitely isn't you. I just give up."

"Don't forget about me."

"I never forget things much any more," Martin said. "And neither will you, if I'm not wrong." He moved as if to set down his guitar, but he did not. She did not set the candle down either. "Well, take care of yourself," he said.

"May joy go with you and peace behind you," she replied.

He turned sharply and went for the last time out of the back screen door, heading west toward the railroad. She watched him go. It was still raining. She put the candle down.

She had no idea what time it was, but the night was far

gone. She turned from the door, humming a slow minor tune. "The winter may go and the spring may die. . . . The summer may fade and the year may fly." September was drawing in the light. Apples, rich and heady, were rotting in the orchard, grapes in the woods. The drought was broken now, and the heat; she could look for frost. Soon she would be able to know every tree for what it was: glass-red sour gums, purple sweet gums, brass-gold tulips and hickories, scarlet-and-orange maples, bright dogwood and brighter sassafras, and oaks in russet and golden-green. Then the subtle, gentle colorings of the wintertime woods and sky. The kitchen would be lit with firelight and snowlight before green-sick spring brightened and ripened into heavy summer once more.

Ashgrove planned to enjoy it all. No one would stop her.

She walked straight out into the rain and right around the fat wild-goose shape of her house. The night was filled with soaking, splattering sounds and smells. Then she decided to brew herself a huge, scalding, and virulently strong pot of tea.

Everything was just as it had been before. Martin had only stayed a little while, and she had been alone a long time before that.

She had told him, when she first met him, "I'll help you get wherever you want to go."

At least she hadn't stopped him from going.

Pumping the water, she sang to herself:

> *"Deep greens and blues*
> *Are the colors I choose;*
> *Won't you let me go down in my dreams? . . ."*

No, that was one of Martin's songs. Try something else. Try an old one.

*"And the grave will deCAY YOU*
*And turn you to dust—*
*Not one boy in a HUNDRED*
*A poor girl can trust.*

*They'll hug you and KISS YOU*
*And tell you more lies*
*Than the crossties on the RAILROAD*
*Or the stars in the sky."*

She did not want to read while she waited for the kettle to boil. She reached for her cards instead. I'm getting to be an addict, she told herself.

She selected certain cards and dealt three times. Then she took the greater trumps and dealt them. Then she spread all seventy-eight cards out all over the top of the table—there was almost not enough room—and examined them scrupulously, holding the candle close.

"I love them."

"I don't like them. What right do cards have to be so sad?"

"Life is sad. So is death."

"What do cards have to do with life or death?"

Prying up a stove lid, she dropped the whole pack into the flames, pushing them down barehanded to make sure they all caught. They took fire slowly, smoldering with a choking odor that she had not expected. The nineteenth-century drawings must have been given some plasticized coating. She watched the pictures twist and wither and ignite: all the kings and queens, knights and pages, greater and lesser trumps, overturned cups and broken towers, and the men and women climbing out of their coffins to hail the Angel of Judgment.

The tea was ready.

Martin was off somewhere, wandering between the crossties and the stars. That was his place.

Ashgrove sat down in the basket chair, clasping her hands around her cup. The mother cat Trilby wandered by, looking askance, called all the kittens, and began to attend to them roughly.

Martin walked through the dark. It was still raining, but that did not bother him much. He would get used to it, as he had got used to just about everything.

He came to the railroad and turned right.

The place called Frazier's Crossing was quiet now, as though no trains had ever stopped there for any reason whatever.

West of here lay the Blue Ridge, then the Great Valley, then the Appalachians. Virginia bordered Kentucky, and Kentucky stretched all the way to Mississippi, halfway across the nation. Well, maybe a third of the way. Virginia had once long ago claimed all that territory, and Kentucky was then known as Kentucky County. Indeed those claims had once reached all the way to the Pacific, when there was nobody there but the Spanish, the Russians, and the Indians. Ashgrove had told him that, hard-core Virginian that she was.

The length and breadth of the country seemed to shrink and foreshorten under his feet, and all its centuries of history seemed very sparse and few.

It would be a lot of walking, but he had all the time in the world; however much time the world had left. He had got along without a map before and he could get along without one now. He knew that alongside the crests of the Blue Ridge ran the Appalachian Trail, which would take you down to Georgia, or north to cross any of the big westbound roads: all the even numbers, the old National

Road and the Lincoln Highway. Even old U.S. 50, which crept through Washington, ended up in San Francisco. There was so much out there. And much would be open to him, though much would be denied.

All right. Fine. Here was the east-west county road. That was a beginning. Martin turned west.

Ginny Reynolds was far too tired and keyed up to sleep. It had quit raining, far on in the night, but the wind was rising. The maple leaves hissed around the dingy windows of Mrs. Franklin's house.

It was so late, such an unreal time of night. Too much had happened. She was still taking it in. The inside of her head was thronged with distorted images of places and people. The Yeargins, the librarian, the minister, all looking aged and troubled. Even Jake Galey looked aged and troubled, though he was probably not much older than she was. And then those others who would never age, no matter what troubles they might have.

What had she got herself into now? She had come to a tentative decision with Howard Yeargin, but she had not signed anything. Perhaps, after all, she was making a horrendous mistake, even though Howard was giving her a fairly good deal.

Maybe one horrendous mistake balances another. I'm going to go back out to the country, watch the sunrise, and see the house in the daylight once more. And see if anyone else is there.

She dressed again in her jeans and muslin blouse and went out to her car. Mrs. Franklin would be disturbed by such comings and goings. Tough on Mrs. Franklin.

She drove down the southbound county road. Far to the west, beyond the railroad, the full moon went down in rags and ruins. At least she would not have to go past that place—crossing—any more, if she did not want to. She pulled the Volkswagen easily into the drive, but in the silence after the rain it made a sound like a threshing machine.

The first landmark Martin came upon was Jake Galey's store. Dim light shone in the upstairs window. He hefted his guitar and went up the outside stairs.

"Who's that?"

"It's me."

"Martin Evans?"

"Yes."

"Do you know what time it is?"

"You're asking me? It's late, is all I know."

"You're wrong. It's early."

"I have to see you a minute."

"You better not make a habit of this."

"I don't plan to."

He discovered Jake to be drinking a popular brand of cheap wine known for no obvious reason as Rose of Tralee, which, as he recalled, tasted of artificial grapes aged in cough-syrup barrels.

"Want some?" Jake offered.

"What is it? Shellac thinner?"

"I'm trying to get to sleep."

"That stuff will give you a head like a herd of wild elephants. You're going to feel like a pile of shit in the morning."

"It already is morning. And I already feel like a pile of shit. It's also going to be Saturday, and I can't take a day off."

"Oh, God," Martin said sympathetically.

"Where's your friend Ashgrove?"

"She said her home is her castle."

"I bet that isn't how she put it."

"That's close enough."

211

"She's crazy," Jake said.

"I told her that a long time ago," Martin said.

"You're crazy too."

"I decided a long time ago that the whole concept of crazy was going to have to be redefined."

"Did you redefine it?"

"I'm still working on it."

"Why don't you just go get her and snatch her out bodily?"

"She *isn't* bodily."

"I see what you mean."

"No, you don't."

They sat there, slouched morosely, Jake on the bed and Martin in the lawn chair. Presently Martin said, "How do you stand that mess?" He meant the Rose of Tralee.

"If it were any good I'd just drink more of it and become a confirmed alcoholic."

Martin did not want to say he saw what Jake meant. "Oh."

"How about some of that last year's dandelion crap?"

"No, thanks. I heard about it already."

"Whatever you heard, it couldn't have been as bad as the reality."

"What happened to your good stuff?"

"I drank it. Haven't made a run to the District lately for more."

Silence again.

Finally Martin said, "What I really came here for was, I want to leave my guitar with you."

"I didn't know you played the guitar."

"Oh, yes."

"Play something."

"No."

"I think you'd better," Jake said. "I think you'll be sorry

if you don't." He said this not threateningly but matter-of-factly.

Martin played the Spanish piece that he had worked on so hard and long.

"I saw the movie that that was used in," Jake said. "*Forbidden Games*. Quite something."

"I didn't see it."

"You can see all the movies you want to now, no trouble at all."

"I'm interested in things more real than movies."

"Movies are real, in a Platonic sense," Jake said. "Though Plato would hardly have thought so." He added, "And you still want to leave that behind?" He meant the guitar.

"After all I said to Ashgrove, and all she said to me, I realized I was getting to be just as crazy as she was. She and her house, me and my guitar; there isn't really that much difference. At least you can haunt a house, but you can't wander the streets with a guitar if people can't see you. At least not if you have any decency or couth. . . . You know. Not scaring people. Unnecessarily. . . . She must have known that the whole time, but she never said anything. I don't know if she was being spiteful or what."

"Ashgrove is babyish and mouthy sometimes, but she's not spiteful. She's so opposed to having her own style cramped that she's unwilling to cramp anybody else's."

He should have known that from the beginning. What in her seemed to alternate between the confidence of a child and the bitchiness of an adult was really total forthrightness, the honesty of someone who has very little left to lose.

He said suddenly, "Do you think it's wrong to want to know about people?"

"Not if you care for them."

"Even if they don't know you know?"

"Depends what you do about it."

"That's it, then," Martin said.

"What are you doing?"

"Slacking the strings."

"Will you be back after this?"

Martin began strapping the guitar up. He shoved it out of sight under the bed, shutting away all that lay between E string and E string. "Don't worry about it if it's too much trouble."

"It's not."

"Do you need anything? Is something wrong?" He had never thought he would ask this of Jake, who usually seemed to be doing all right.

"Nothing permanent."

"Maybe things will work out," Martin said hesitantly, feeling this about covered everything.

"Maybe."

"Thanks for everything."

"It's okay."

"No, it isn't, but thanks anyway."

"Good luck, Martin."

Jake poured himself another glass of Rose of Tralee. "Maybe this one will do it," he said. Martin let himself out.

Sometime after the rain had stopped, Ashgrove heard the clatter and chug of a four-cylinder engine pulling into her drive. Jake, she thought, and got up to meet him, taking what was left of the candle. But it was the sorrel-haired woman named Ginny Reynolds, striding through the wet grass as though she owned the place.

Which maybe she did.

How can I get her to leave? Maybe I can talk her out of
it.

Ratsbane.

They peered at each other through the back screen
door.

"Can I come in?"

"Did you want to?"

"Yes. Please."

Ashgrove held the door and Ginny took a chair.
Ashgrove sat across the table on the other chair, straddling
it in a pose that made her feel defensive and aggressive at
the same time.

Ginny sniffed. "What's burning? Doesn't smell too
good."

"Trash. Are you going to buy my house?"

"No. I don't have enough money."

"My."

"Mr. Yeargin says he'll rent it to me, though. He hopes
in a year or so the talk will die down and he can sell it for
what it's really worth."

"Is that all he believes it was? Just talk?"

"He has to believe that. He isn't equipped to deal with
any alternative. His wife believes it was more than that.
She still gets quite moved when she talks about you."

"Oh," Ashgrove groaned.

"You really satisfied some kind of need with her. For
excitement, for someone to care for—I don't know. She
invited me for coffee. She wants to be friends. . . . Maybe
he'll be nicer to her now, realize how lonely she was. I
don't know about that either."

"What about me and what I need? I need my house, and
nobody wants to let me have it."

"I'll let you have it. I just want some of it. You seem
fairly tolerable."

"*Merci beaucoup*," Ashgrove said, outraged.

"Surely we can stay out of each other's way. I'm so tired. I don't think Joe will come back. Do you? He didn't sound as though he'd darken the door again."

Ashgrove started to say, yes, she certainly did think he'd be back any minute, but her heart was not in making up a big story.

They both knew nothing like that was likely to recur any time soon, anyway.

"Where's the other one—Martin?" Ginny continued. "How does he feel about all this?"

"How he feels is, he left."

"Oh. Was that my fault?"

"No. Oh, no. He was going to anyway. I wouldn't stop him. He said he wasn't going to stay in one place, and I said, well, I was. So he went out that door, just a little while ago. What's purple and migratory? Martin the grape. Did you pass him on the road?"

"Not that I noticed. . . . So you miss him already."

It was none of Ginny's business, but Ashgrove was half talking to herself. "I didn't think that I would. I thought just to have known him would be enough—that these things sort of exist outside time. But they don't."

"No. They don't."

"You wouldn't guess what he was like, to look at him. He looked very quiet and serious."

"What are you going to do about it?"

"Stay right here. I certainly deserve it, after all that I've been through."

"Well, I feel the same way, and I'm going to stay right here with you."

"Well, I wish you wouldn't."

"You may be some sort of little tiny ghost person, but I find you more tolerable than my landlady or my boy-friend."

216

"I don't want to hear about your landlady or your boyfriend. Go away."

"This is going to be exactly like the Arab-Israeli war." Ginny sighed. She kicked off her sandals under the table.

"Well, I'll be the Israelis," Ashgrove said belligerently. "*Havah Nagilah.*" Then she cried, "Oh! Woe is me! Nothing is funny any more. It isn't even any fun to be ugly! I miss him too much! He put a curse on me. That's exactly what he did. I'm being haunted. He said I probably wouldn't forget anything, and I haven't, and I bet I never will."

"You will," Ginny said.

"How do you know?"

"Because I'm older than you, and I've forgotten a lot."

"Well, that doesn't help me at all. . . . I cannot weep, nor answer have I none, But what should go by water. If you know what I mean."

"No, I don't," Ginny said sharply, "and I doubt you do either."

"Oh, I do, but it would take way too long to explain."

"Ashgrove."

"What?"

"I really wish I could help you."

"People are always saying that to me. Or I'm always saying it to them. Well. I suppose you're here now. I've been ugly for so long. I might as well be polite. Do you want to see the rest of the house?"

"Yes, I do."

"This, as you see, is the kitchen. The stove really takes some understanding." Then her control broke down again. "This is my kitchen! I don't want to share it! I don't want you coming in and putting up smily faces and spice-and-herb charts all over the place. I can't go through with this!"

"I couldn't care less about spices and herbs, or smily

faces. You can do all the cooking. It will be like having a roommate."

Ashgrove hauled up her heaviest artillery. "What do you pregnant ladies like to eat?"

"Is that relevant?" Ginny asked mildly, not twitching a muscle.

"I think it is, if you're going to walk into my house and promptly deliver a child."

"Not promptly. It will be a few more months."

"People keep telling me I'm crazy. I don't think I'm the only one. How can you take on a house at a time like this?"

"Sometimes I think I'm crazy too. Other times I just think everything worth having has to be dearly bought."

"So do some things that aren't worth having. The question is which are which."

"Yes. That is the question."

"Well, you may be crazy, but you're sort of brave," Ashgrove said. She was beginning to decide that in spite of herself she liked Ginny, whose undemanding serenity was almost catching. "But what are you going to do? Who's going to help you?"

"With the baby?"

"Yes. It's a long haul to the hospital, if I remember rightly, and I do."

"I'm not worried about that. Well, I am," Ginny corrected herself, "but not about getting there. I'm big-boned and there's a lot of muscle on me. It'll take me awhile. Most of the women in my family are like that."

"I suggest you call Jake if you need anything."

"Jake Galey?"

"The same. He's one of my oldest friends and best neighbors."

"You think he'd come?"

"Yes, I do. He's like that."

"It's a thought." She didn't say what kind of thought it was.

"Martin and I got in some wood, but you'll need more if you don't plan to do a lot of fixing up."

"I might put in a bottled-gas stove anyway."

"Want me to show you about this one?"

"Maybe later. I should've gone to bed long ago. I'm dying on my feet. Excuse me."

"Quite all right. It's better to die on your feet than to live on your knees, or something like that. Want me to fix you some coffee?"

"Thanks."

"You won't believe this in the morning."

"Yes, I will. I've believed weirder. And look." She blew the flattening candle out. "It is morning."

"The casement slowly grows a glimmering square."

"Whatever."

"Well. Now this is the firebox, and this is the damper, and this is where you take the ashes out, and throw them on the ash heap, next to the compost. You have to keep this thing clean. From partial fires the waste remains and kills, if you know what I mean. It's really not unlike Martin's beast. You should've been here when he got that thing going. . . . Of course you can get the electric turned back on; then you won't have to wear yourself out pumping."

"Have you got anything to eat?" Ginny asked suddenly. "I'd love something on my stomach."

"Afraid not, except cat food."

Ginny searched her purse till she located a battered cellophane packet of soda crackers. She munched them down, not waiting for her coffee. Hearing the crunching, one of the cats came charging up. It was Brandenburg, the cat who was fool enough to love everybody.

"Cats are attractive, ornamental, nice to have around,

out for what they can get, and not a bit of help when you're in trouble," Ashgrove declared.

"You're talking about the man I love," Ginny said, propping her elbow on the table.

Ashgrove would very much have liked to ask more about the man Ginny loved. But she denied herself the privilege. She asked instead, "How do you feel about cats?"

"Oh, I like cats, even though, as you say, they're real bandits. I couldn't have any at Franklin's. She had a phobia about pee and other bodily excretions."

"I was wondering, would you take care of mine? You can get their food from Jake; he has the kind they like."

"How many do you have?"

"Well, eight in all, but four are little. There they are. See? They're asleep. Pyracantha and Tom must be out somewhere."

"I see."

"I've already had them for the cutest part of their lives," Ashgrove said. "They are so pretty. But they really like places better than people."

"The territorial instinct," Ginny said.

Ashgrove said, "Ahhh," spreading her hand out on the back of the chair as she stood at the stove. "Well, there's territory and territory."

The coffee was ready. She poured Ginny some. The forgotten wineglass and Scrabble tiles still cluttered the table.

"Don't you ghosts drink coffee?"

"Not exactly."

"Do you ever sleep?"

"Sometimes."

"Can you have sex? . . . It would sure be the ideal setup."

"I just don't think I want to talk about it."

"You're angry. I shouldn't have asked all that."

"No. I'm thinking. I thought things could always be the

same, but they're not. They never will be. I don't like change. I don't like for things and people to change."

"Nobody does, but it's the name of the game."

"I thought I was past all that, but I wasn't, and Martin wasn't either."

"Ashgrove, the way you keep talking about Martin, you'd better go and find him, if it isn't too late."

"That's just what worries me. If I were sure it was too late, I'd feel better. You know?"

"Yes, I know."

"I keep thinking that he hasn't gone far, though I'm not just sure where he's got to. Also I keep thinking he'll come back. He might come back. He knows where this house is."

Ginny said nothing. Ashgrove was quiet too, for a while. Then she said, "Maybe that's what Francie Lee thought."

"Who's Francie Lee?"

"My mother."

"Oh."

"And she waited half her life for my father to come back, or something."

"Did she get it?"

"She finally left. Out flew the web and floated wide, the mirror cracked from side to side. But I can't just jump because old Martin said Frog, and ask how high on the way up."

"But you'll never find out how high, if you don't. Go on. I'll take care of your cats. The house will still be here if you decide to come back. To that extent, nothing will have changed."

"Except me," Ashgrove said unhappily.

She turned toward the breezeway door. Ginny Reynolds took a grateful draft of strong black coffee.

"I'll tell you one more thing," Ashgrove said. "My

amaryllis is out back, a big fat ugly-looking bulb. It's about died off now, but on New Year's Day you give it a big drink of water and by March you'll have the biggest red flower you ever saw."

"I should be needing a big red flower about that time," Ginny said. "Thanks."

Ashgrove still strove for an exit line.

If Martin comes, you tell him I've been here and gone.

No. Once more she denied herself a privilege. She replied to Ginny, "Oh! Thank you. And don't try to bring in that avocado tub, it's too heavy for you."

She went out the breezeway door and up to the main part of the house. She left by the front door, leaving it standing wide. Then she doubled back, heading west toward Frazier's Crossing.

It was just coming day. In a few more minutes you would be able to see the colors of the world, the trees turning green before you and, behind you, silhouetted black against the sunrise. Ashgrove ran lightly over the uneven ground, once in a while glancing over her shoulder to see if the sun had cleared the edge of the world, and to take one more look at the orchard, and the chimneys of her house beyond its hedges and trees. That was a good fire she had kindled in the stove. Its smoke still rose sweetly from the kitchen chimney, and steam from the long night's rain drifted off the fields.

The northbound passenger train had already passed. But there at the grade crossing on the county road Martin still leaned against the crossbuck, empty-handed, and free to do anything he chose. Free just to stand here and watch trains.

It was going to be a gorgeous day. The sky was immaculate, baked-enamel blue, dusted around the horizon with gold bloom. Asters, tassel-headed and sun-faced, bloomed at the road's edge. The trees, cleansed of their dust to greenness again, looked almost like full-blown summer, but the grasses were pale in the fields, the sumac and sassafras were reddening in the ditch, and far overhead the change was beginning, the cold air from Canada wiping the sky clean, polishing its blue, and breathing a hint of frost.

The electrical signal began shrieking again. The gates came down. Here was yet another train, a southbound freight. It clanked and rumbled by, pounding iron from New York to New Orleans. Its cars spoke of east and west and all points in between. D. T. & I., E. J. & E., G. M. & O.—Southern, Southern, Santa Fe, Frisco—L. & N., the Dixie Line, Central of Georgia, State of Maine.

In the midst of all the clangor and pandemonium, a quiet, pleased, familiar voice said at his elbow, "It's a mighty rough road from Lynchburg to Danville."

"And lyin' on a three-mile grade," Martin replied.

They looked at one another. Daylight fell sharply on their faces and left them the way it found them: pale, slightly sardonic, and caught in youth forever, as far as anyone knew.

They smiled for the first time in some while.

Martin said, "Took you a while to get here."

"Oh, yes! Forever!" Ashgrove said.

WATERLOO HIGH SCHOOL LIBRARY
1464 INDUSTRY RD.
ATWATER, OHIO  44201

If anything
Swearingen, Martha

12986
Fic Swe